S0-BNY-053

SILENT STARSONG

T.J. Wooldridge

T.J. Wooldridge

SPENCER HILL
MIDDLE GRADE

Copyright © 2014 by T.J. Wooldridge

Sale of the paperback edition of this book without its cover is unauthorized.

Spencer Hill Middle Grade

This book is a work of fiction. Names, characters, places, and incidents are products of the author's imagination or are used fictitiously. Any resemblance to actual events, locales, or persons, living or dead, is entirely coincidental.

All rights reserved, including the right to reproduce this book or portions thereof in any form whatsoever.
Contact: Spencer Hill Middle Grade, an imprint of Spencer Hill Press, PO Box 247, Contoocook, NH 03229, USA

Please visit our website at www.spencerhillmiddlegrade.com

First Edition: July 2014.
T.J. Wooldridge
Silent Starsong : a novel / by T.J. Wooldridge – 1st ed.
p. cm.

Summary:
Eleven-year-old girl and her alien friend defy their families and cultures who say they are "not good enough" and search for their destinies in the songs of stars.

The author acknowledges the copyrighted or trademarked status and trademark owners of the following wordmarks mentioned in this fiction:
Thermos

Cover design and illustration by Veronica Jones
Interior illustrations by Slake Saunders
Interior layout by Jennifer Carson and Marie Romero

ISBN 978-1-939392-93-0 (paperback)
ISBN 978-1-939392-94-7 (e-book)

Printed in the United States of America

To Scott,
for believing in Kyra's, Marne's, and my songs.
All my love, always.

To Del,
for being an awesome "godmom" to Kyra and Marne.

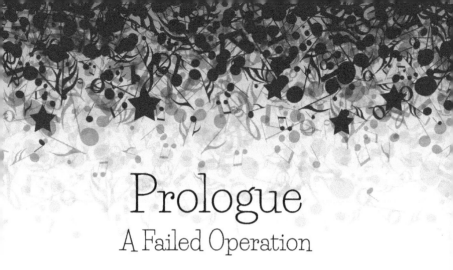

Prologue
A Failed Operation

ONE YEAR AGO...

7 Messidor 896

We're back on the electrotram, and Daddy didn't even give me the window seat. He's sadder about this than I am. Daddy's face says he's expecting to get yelled at when we get home.

Mom will be very angry. I'll get sent to my room and they'll yell... and I'll be able to feel it upstairs. I guess Daddy needs the window seat. It's pretty outside, and he's leaning on the window, staring as the flat, dry grasses and orange sky fly by. Daddy showed me on his tablet that the electrotram can go almost 200 miles per hour. I also read that it makes almost no noise, which doesn't affect me, anyway.

At the hospital, I was in a room with a boy named Bran. His operation had worked, and he was just getting an adjustment because he got better. He was nice to me and wrote on a whiteboard with eraser markers and gave me a flower when the doctor came in to talk to my dad. I saw his face fall when the doctor said my surgery didn't work. But I already knew it didn't work. Nothing had changed; I still couldn't hear. ~~I probably won't ever get to hear.~~

1

Bran was nice except for the part about the gelatin. I like gelatin. I only get it if I'm sick, and the hospital had blue gelatin, which tasted really good. He wrote me a note that said, "Do you know what that's made from?" He had a weird smile and I shook my head no, so he wrote, "The hooves of dead eqcannuses."

I made a face and wrote on my napkin that he was a liar. He shook his head. Then I wrote, "How do they run without hooves?"

He answered, "They don't have to run; they're dead." I made a face at him, and he wrote some more. "If they get hurt or sick or get born wrong they send them to a slaughterhouse where they get killed and their hooves become gelatin." I asked what happened to the rest of their body and he shrugged and wrote, "Food for other things?" I made another face at him, but my gelatin treat was ruined.

The doctor's notes, which I made Dad show me on his tablet even though he didn't want me to see them, said I was permanently deformed. I think it is a good thing that I am not an eqcannus or I could be food for something else.

Her father gently tugged the corner of her journal and Kyra snapped it shut, looking up defensively. He held up both hands as she pointed to the cover, which read, "Diary." The corner of his mouth twitched in amusement as he tucked a stray lock of her light-brown hair behind her ear. "Big secrets at nine years old?" he signed to her.

She smiled back. Her dad had gotten them a book from the library about secret hand codes. It was in the children's section, but he had told her that, on his home planet, people who couldn't hear used similar signs. It became their own secret code. "Maybe. What are we going to tell Mom?" she signed back, and rested against his side as he put an arm around her shoulders.

"Don't worry about it, love. That's another sixteen hours away. Try to sleep."

"I slept a long time after the…" She paused, not knowing the sign for "operation," and pointed to her ears instead.

Her father shrugged; he didn't know it either. "I did not sleep. I waited awake the whole time to make sure you were all right."

Kyra raised one eyebrow. "Did you think I would hear less than nothing?"

Her father looked at her, his clear blue eyes still quite sad. "No. But all…" He paused and then spelled out "'o-p-e-r-a-t-i-o-n-s' are dangerous. You might not have woken up, or you could have been in pain or… I don't know."

She looked at her father for several minutes, trying to read between his expression and the gestures of his hands. Kyra sensed there was more there that she wasn't reading. Biting her lip, she scooted to her knees and kissed him on the cheek. "I'm all right," she signed with a big smile.

He laughed; she liked the face he made when he was laughing. He hugged her, kissing her forehead. "You are more than all right, my darling girl. You are amazing."

Chapter 1
What Happens to the Unwanted?

Ten-year-old Kyra flinched as her mother tapped her head with a box. She turned so she could see what her mother was asking. Zalana held up the gelatin carton. "Want some?" her lips said. The girl looked over her shoulder into the casino room, where a wall-screen displayed six-legged *eqcannuses* running around a track. Napoleon's Central Supermart boasted five levels of shopping for "all your needs." There were three salons and four gambling lounges that sported wall-screens for various events, including the popular derbies for the carnivorous, hoofed beasts. Inside this lounge, well-dressed men and women jumped around, waving slips of paper. Kyra's eyes were drawn to the *eqcannuses* following a rabbit on a stick. Occasionally, a camera would catch a close-up of a white-spittled, toothy muzzle or a wild dark eye with an elliptical pupil.

Two side screens showed the news, one for the planet Cordelier and one for interstellar coverage. No one paid

4

those much attention, despite the concerned faces of the newscasters as the scroll below them announced that an InterGalactic Travel cruise ship had been fired upon by United Foundation Consortium terrorists.

Her mother rapped her a little harder. "Kyra! Do you want this or not?"

She winced from the vibrations and knew her mother was impatient. She shook her head and lowered her eyes. It had been almost a year since she'd eaten gelatin. Not since the last operation to fix her hearing had failed. Not since Bran, the boy in the hospital, told her it was made from the hooves of *eqcannuses* who were not good enough to race.

Zalana threw up her hands and returned the box of gelatin to the shelf. She huffed down the aisle, and Kyra jogged to stay close. Her mother's mouth was moving, but she couldn't see it well enough to know what she was saying. Even if she were looking straight on, she probably wouldn't understand. Her mother usually spoke too fast for her to comprehend. Daddy had only recently begun teaching her to match lip movements with the hand signs he'd taught her before and with written words.

As her mother paused to compare the prices of vacuum-sealed vegetables, Kyra watched one of the small news screens off to the side of the jumping-people-filled gambling lounge. Three news speakers sat around a table, one of them a woman with the metallic hair and eyes of someone from the planet Caterbree, while the other two looked more like the humans on Cordelier. The man had dark-brown skin with white and grey hair in tight curls close to his face, while the other woman had pale skin, with dark hair and eyes. They were talking about the incident with the IGT cruise ship. Fortunately, reading had always been something Kyra was quite good at, so she easily followed the fast-moving, color-coded closed-caption scrolls at the bottom of the screen. They were talking about questioning the captured terrorists, and if they would be questioned on Cordelier, the planet that owned the cruise ship, or Caterbree, which governed the space they were captured in.

The Caterbreian woman had just asked whether the UFC was an "actual" threat to anyone when Kyra felt her baby sister, Alyce, start to fuss. The fussing felt like a liquid itch spreading across her neck, over her shoulders, and down into her hands, the places where she was always the most sensitive to sounds and vibration. Turning to look at Alyce, Kyra saw the one-year-old wrinkling her reddening face toward their mom, who was also turning away from the screen. Mom's face, normally a golden-pink color, was pale, and the line between her eyebrows grew deeper as she rolled the carriage back and forth to calm Alyce.

Once the baby calmed, Zalana cut her gaze to Kyra and frowned more. "Come on. We need to meet your dad at the register and see what we've been assigned for water rations. It's getting late."

Kyra nodded. She wanted to ask her mother about the newscast, why it had made her so angry and scared. She didn't, though. She had a hard time talking with her mother, who wasn't learning the hand-signs very well, and even if her mother did know the signs, Kyra wasn't sure she knew how to put together a question that could match the ill feeling in her stomach. It was easier to just look at the colorful boxes and bags of sealed fruits, vegetables, and fresh grains against the perfectly white surroundings.

Her eyes fell on the slow-moving machines that moved up and down everything, always cleaning. Reaching her hand toward two nearby ones, she noticed the hum from the large machine on the floor felt different from that of the small machine scooting on the shelves around the products. She considered pausing to touch them the way her dad had often had her touch pieces of machines he would take apart and put back together, but Mom had picked up her pace as she headed for the register. Kyra pulled her hand away from the machine and ran to catch up.

At the register, her dad was waving a sheet of green paper that listed their water rations for the week. He always took care of those while her mother shopped, because of the long lines. Even with Mom being a Starbard, an important job on many planets, the family had to wait in line like everyone else to purchase their water each week.

"Hghai!" she called to her dad as she waved back. Kyra ignored the pained look on her mother's face. Her dad had recently started to teach her how to speak properly, but Kyra was having a much harder time with it than with reading, writing, or signing.

Kyra started to run to her father, but her mother's hand came down hard on her shoulder. She let out another noise, this time unintentionally, and looked up, pain summoning tears. Zalana gasped and let go quickly. "I'm sorry, my heart! I forgot... It's just you shouldn't run off!"

Pouting, Kyra waited for her dad, who wove through the crowds toward them, ration sheet clutched tightly. He wrapped one arm around her mother's waist and planted a kiss on her lips, then moved to Alyce and covered her little face with kisses until she laughed. Kyra liked it when Alyce laughed; the sensation it caused felt like bubbles tickling Kyra's skin.

Finally, Nicolas squatted in front of his older daughter and kissed both her cheeks. Looking at Zalana, he asked, "Mind if I kidnap her before the outdoor market ships close? It's the last day of the season—"

Her mother said something that looked like she was scolding her dad. Kyra could read his lips saying "I know, love" before smiling sweetly. Her mother's expression softened some, but not entirely. There was less of a harsh vibration in her response, but she still spoke too fast for Kyra to read much more than "money" and "foretell" and her sister's name. Kyra got the gist, though. It was her parents' usual argument. Well, her mother's usual argument. Alyce was born with the Starbard mark, and even though Kyra was too, her sister could hear, so the family needed to make sure money was spent on Alyce, since Alyce would have to carry on the line.

The argument always made Kyra feel sick in her stomach.

As he turned away from her mom, Kyra figured her dad felt almost the same from the expression on his face. But when he looked down at her, everything changed, and he gave her a big smile. Twirling her around, he tickled under her arms as she spun. She couldn't help but giggle.

He grinned at her. "I like it when you laugh. You don't do it nearly enough," he said, speaking slowly and forming the words carefully.

She laughed again and blew a kiss. He picked her up, swung her around, and put her down. "You're getting heavy," he signed to her. "Not such a little girl anymore!"

She gave him a sweet smile and batted her eyelashes, which made him laugh.

"I have a surprise for you, Kyra, but we have to hurry." He took her hand and slowly jogged around the multicolored tents and streamers of the Darlinian Outdoor Market, which set up in the fields behind the Central Supermart for the first month of every season, just as the weather changed.

Nicolas pulled his longish black hair out of his face as the sharp wind whipped it around. Kyra looked up at him in his thin silk shirt and pulled her maroon coat more closely around her neck and shoulders. Still, the cold pins of the coming winter touched her skin. Her father hardly ever got chilled, even in the winter months when winds blew so hard they swayed the tall pillars holding up the electrotram's single rail. The first time she'd noticed the swaying, she'd asked him if the tram would fall, and he'd explained that the pillars were made of a metal that would hold up in the wind, and that the energy making the tram run also kept it from falling.

She wondered if there were an energy holding down the metal pegs that kept the market tents from flying away like giant birds or butterflies. The ropes strained in the wind, making the pegs and ropes look like they were holding down those flying monsters that had lived on Cordelier before people settled here, according to her history books. Neither of Kyra's parents had ever taken her past the tents, in which merchants sold pretty clothes, food, and toys from other parts of the planet. Some tents even held puppet shows in the mornings.

As they left the colorful tents, she gasped as what looked like a small city of metal and glass buildings with wings spread out beyond the merchant tents and across the dry-grass field.

Her dad tapped her upper arm. "Those are starships, small ones," he told her.

She looked at him in confusion.

"Star. Ships. Your mom goes on bigger ones for some of her foretellings on other planets."

Kyra blinked as she digested this information. Other planets. Her dad was from another planet, one that was colder than their home planet, Cordelier. She knew her mom would often be gone for months for a foretelling on another planet. Slowly, she nodded. He nodded back and rubbed her arms. "We're meeting someone, from another planet far away. We need to hurry, though."

After nodding again, Kyra struggled to keep up with her dad's quick stride. He clasped her hand tightly, making it a little sore in his effort to keep her close.

Some of the starships opened up on one side, with tents or giant awnings covering part of the ship but revealing tables full of things inside, like one of the smaller shops inside the Supermart—only darker and definitely not pristine white. Other ships just had rows of tables with no covering or protection from the wind, and still others had small collections of tents set up outside. Metal coils and machine parts were openly displayed. Fresh fruit or meat or fish (some with thin clouds of hovering flies and smells that made Kyra wrinkle her nose) sat in baskets in other shops. And some of the places had mostly-closed flaps, keeping people from seeing any merchandise. Many of the people selling things looked dirty, and some smelled almost as bad as the unusual fruits and meats. Most wore the trouser-blouse fashions Kyra saw on native Cordelierans (covered with heavy coats, of course); others wore jumpsuits or dresses and coats that looked like liquid metal—but dulled, as if in need of polishing. Some wore tattered woolen blankets and robes in layers; others looked like they wore the skins of animals!

More than half the people she saw selling things were the humans that lived across the majority of planets that she knew of, but she also recognized aliens with deep blue skin, and those who looked like they were part bird. Some beings that she'd never seen before had odd growths or shapes on their heads or faces, and pure silver eyes. A few of the shopkeepers—human *and* alien—leered at her as she passed. So did some of the other shoppers, nearly all of whom were human. Kyra remembered that since Cordelier, of all the populated planets, had the fewest livable areas, few aliens chose to settle there, even after humans had made it habitable.

She glanced up a few times; her father appeared nervous as he barreled straight ahead. After a moment, he broke into a jog, yanking her arm as she raced to keep up.

He called to a bearded human man, dressed in layers of wool blankets, who was exiting the starship they approached. The man raised an eyebrow at them and made a face Kyra couldn't read, but that made her father tighten his hand. She made a noise and wiggled free of his grip, rubbing her palm. He mouthed "Sorry" and "Stay close" and returned to talking with the man. The man seemed to mumble; she couldn't comprehend his lip movements. After a few seconds of this exchange, she grew bored and looked around.

Stacked by the starship, not very far from where her father was speaking to the man, were cages about as tall as Alyce, and each enclosed a single alien animal unlike anything Kyra had seen before. Granted, she didn't leave the house often, and she'd seen lots of things just on this short walk that she'd never seen before. However, these little creatures intrigued her. They stood on two legs, and many gripped the cage bars with two small hands. Black button eyes glistened like jewels from oval heads, wider than tall. Their skins were various shades of purple and lavender. Some had spindly appendages hanging limp from their necks. The setting sun cast shadows that made it hard to discern more details about these strange creatures, but one stood out from the rest.

Not purple or lavender, this creature was bright pink. Kyra glanced over her shoulder. Her dad was waiting for the man to check his currency card, so she slipped around the table and headed toward the stacked cages. Squatting by the pink thing, she curiously looked it in the eye.

It had no nose, but it did have a single slit below its eyes that could be a mouth. The pink flesh stretched smoothly across the entire head. Atop the head were antenna-type protrusions, small ones, with knobs on the top. They leaned slightly in her direction. Watching them move took her aback; it was like watching slugs crawl.

Its small hands, almost as small as her baby sister's hands, clenched the bars as it looked at her. Warily, she stuck out her forefinger to touch them. Upon feeling the soft skin, she quickly snatched her hand back, in case it should bite her. It blinked shiny black eyes the size of the small round stones between the plants in her family's back gardens. She winced again, wondering from where the lids came; she saw no wrinkles or folds.

~I won't bite you.~

Kyra gasped and stumbled onto her butt. Her mind swam with a hundred thousand thoughts, but one stuck out the most. *Did I just hear?!*

~Technically, no. Not in your species' sense of hearing, anyway.~

Kyra pressed her fist to her mouth and bit her knuckles. Her throat vibrated in reaction. What was this thing? Did it have magic? Could it make her hear?

~Now you've gone and done it,~ it said, sounding both angry and sad. ~I don't know what they'll do with me now that I've gone and scared you.~

Her dad was by her side, and she felt his raised voice as she looked up at him.

"—do you think you're doing? I told you to stay by me! You have no idea!"

Her dad's expression looked more scared than she'd ever seen it, but the shock of that didn't surpass that of possibly hearing. Gaping between her dad and the thing, she began to sign rapidly: "Can hear! The thing talked to me! I can hear it!"

~I *told* you, it's not really hearing. You're just predisposed to telepathy.~

"Look." Her father helped her up, brushing the yellow grass and dirt off the back of her coat and pink trousers. "Maybe this isn't such a good idea… Let's go, Kyra."

She shook her head. Something told her that this thing, like all of them, was scared. They all got scared when the other man came over with her dad. She pointed at the pink thing again and tugged on her ear. It looked from her, to her father, and to the bearded man. It didn't want to go with the bearded man.

"Kyra, sweetheart…" her father began, glancing at the thing as well.

Biting her lip, she signed, "Ask him what happens to these things. Where does he take them? Where do they come from? They're scared of him."

Her dad frowned but spoke to the man in mumbles.

~They're speaking Kurduxtian. You probably don't know it,~ the thing said. Kyra looked back at it, heart pounding as her mind jumped to *eqcannuses* and gelatin.

Her father tapped her arm. "They just keep going around to different planets until they all find homes."

Kyra frowned and signed, "What if they do not find homes on any planet?"

Her father opened his mouth and closed it, then shrugged without meeting her eyes. Kyra folded her arms impatiently. He shrugged again.

~He knows. So do you. He just doesn't want to tell you.~ Its "voice" carried feeling—anger, sadness, and other emotions Kyra recognized but hadn't names for.

Tightening her lips, she pointed to the thing again. She signed, "You brought me here to see if I could hear them, correct? I can hear that one. It can help me…so Mom is not so…so Mom likes me more."

Her father lowered his eyes. "Your mother loves you and you know it," he signed emphatically. Kyra didn't budge. He turned back to the man, and they mumbled some more as she squatted next to the thing.

"What's your name?" she signed.

~Marne,~ it said. ~And you can just think what you want me to know.~ It leaned toward her while its antennae turned toward where her father and the man were speaking with big gestures.

~Do you know what they're saying?~ she tried to think at it.

~They're negotiating my price.~

She paused and then asked her next question. ~What are you?~

She couldn't see any pupils but she got the distinct feeling it had turned its eyes upon her. ~I'm a he, in your language, not an *it* or a *thing*, first off. And I'm a Naratsset.~

~Oh. He. Sorry. Naratsset… Are you from a different planet?~

~Why? Are there Naratssets on this planet?~

She frowned. He "sounded"…something she wasn't familiar with. ~Well, you're here on this planet. You could be from one of the countries I haven't been in, yet. There's a lot of those.~

He blinked again and shook his head a little. ~Yes, I'm from another planet. Natarasq is about 500,000 light-years away from here.~

~Light-years?~

~The distance light can travel in a year? Well, not a year *here* on this planet, but wherever a year is on whatever planet the term originated from...which is a long way away.~

~Oh.~ Kyra wanted to ask Marne several more questions, but her father brushed her shoulder again. She looked up to read his lips.

"He's yours. Let's go before your mother starts to worry."

Kyra smiled, feeling her throat vibrate with her happiness. Marne looked at her oddly. The bearded man moved the cages, picked up Marne's, and handed it to Nicolas.

"Do we have to keep him in the cage? He doesn't like it," Kyra signed.

"At least until we get home," he replied, looking at the Naratsset warily as they walked back through the market. Around them, people were closing starship doors and securing tent flaps.

The lights dimmed, making the walk even darker as the sun set.

"His name..." She wasn't sure how to spell it in signs.

"Marne," the pink alien said. She still "heard" it, but the slit of his mouth fluttered this time.

Her father nearly dropped the cage. Kyra smiled. "None of them said anything while we were there!" he said defensively.

"We're not allowed."

"Oh," he replied, looking between Marne and Kyra, who could hardly tear her eyes from the alien to watch her father's lips. "I see."

Kyra giggled and her father smiled. She signed, "I can hear him though he says I am not hearing... What is it?"

"Telepathy. All Naratssets are telepathic...and Kyra has a predisposition for it," Marne said.

Her dad blinked at Marne and looked between him and Kyra once more. "Naratsset," he muttered.

"Ratsi is what the traders call us...as an insult."

Kyra frowned. "That's mean!" she signed.

Marne shrugged.

"Please, don't go into my mind like that," her father said, face looking strained and eyes narrowed at Marne. "And perhaps we should cut this conversation short. I don't think your mother... She'll need...to talk about this."

Kyra's smile faded as she looked at the little thing. ~Mom's going to be angry,~ she explained.

Marne just nodded his head and sat down in his small cage. Kyra's stomach tightened...and she thought she felt his worry as well. He didn't say it, but she sensed he was afraid to go back. She didn't blame him, though she feared he wouldn't like it with her much more.

~I think I'll like you,~ came his thought.

She was about to reply, but then cringed as she felt her mother's furious yelling wash over her. Covering her shoulders with her hands, since that seemed to dull the discomfort, she ducked behind her father.

Marne looked at her with his black stone eyes. ~I think we'll be all right, though, really.~ At least Marne sounded more confident than she felt.

When Kyra met Marne.

Chapter 2
Vibrational Discord

Kyra still wanted to know what they were saying. Marne sensed her curiosity and looked at the human girl with eyes as green as this planet's summer leaves. She hugged her shoulders on the bed. She lay on her side, and a small line of light illuminated a diagonal across her pale and expressive face. No wonder so few humans learned telepathy; the lines and contours of their heads showed all their thoughts, fears, and emotions. With a sigh, he turned back to the door.

He didn't want to share this part. Obviously, Zalana knew a thing or two about "Ratsis" that Nicolas didn't.

"So, you spent all of our savings on a defective alien? That's just wonderful. Just like everything else we've done—useless!"

"Z, you don't mean that!"

"I don't know anymore. Alyce needs us, too. She can carry on the gift, anyway."

"So can Kyra! She has the mark, darker than any recorded, right? And her sensitivity. Shoulders, hands, just *more*. You've always been like that—"

"For sake of the sacred, Nicolas, she's *deaf,* and there's nothing anyone or anything can do about it! She can't hear the stars, so how can she foretell?"

"Maybe she does it differently—a special way that we just don't know about yet!"

~Marne! What are they saying?~

Kyra had picked up telepathic communication within a few hours, down to even getting a "whine" into her communication.

~Your mother's angry about the money your father spent on me, because she wants to spend some on your sister, too.~

The girl didn't reply, but Marne got the distinct feeling she knew he wasn't saying everything. She was hurt. He didn't like that feeling coming from her, so he continued.

~I'm pink. We're supposed to be blue; the darker the blue, the better we are. I'm...well, that's why I was on the ship; I'm...~ He paused. ~I'm defective.~

Kyra made another off-key noise in her throat and crept out of bed and over to him. Her arms were around him before he realized what she was doing, and he instinctively emitted a electric-like shock.

She yipped, then jammed her fist in her mouth to keep from making more noise, looking at him with huge eyes as she backed toward her bed.

Marne pressed up against the wall, just as frightened. He tilted one antenna toward the door; the two adults still argued. ~What did you just do?~ he asked—even as she demanded, ~What was that for? That hurt!~

~You surprised me. You grabbed me.~ He relaxed some.

~I was going to hug you.~ She still projected hurt feelings. ~The doctors said I was a defect, and I couldn't be fixed…that's what else she said, wasn't it?~

Marne looked at her for a few moments. ~To "hug" me?~

~A hug. Don't you hug on your planet?~

~I don't think so. Usually if someone bigger is wrapping their arms around you, it's a bad thing.~

Kyra paused. ~Oh. I was trying to be nice.~

~I understand that now.~ He turned back to the door. ~They got quieter.~

~Did Mom say…~

~Not as bad as you put it. She's more angry about the money.~

~They spent lots of money on me…to fix my ears, and they had savings for emergencies that they've had to use for bills sometimes.~

~That's what it sounded like.~ He looked back at her. ~And you don't need to be fixed. You're fine like you are; most humans can't communicate like this…and you picked up my thoughts right away, and I was hardly meaning to send them.~

~Oh.~

She didn't seem convinced. He heard small rustles of movement as she crept back into bed. Air hissed from the slit of his mouth as he sighed, a mannerism he'd picked up from previous owners, and from the humans who'd carted him and the other "defects" around for more time than he cared to keep track of. Even if he could have done the math for all the space-travel time and planet time.

~They stopped yelling, at least,~ she thought to him.

~Yes, they did. But they're still talking, and they don't sound happy either.~

~I won't let them take you back.~

He laughed dryly and stopped when he sensed her confusion at his mood. ~I don't think you could stop them, though I appreciate it. Besides, my seller was leaving the planet tonight. Your parents can't get their money back... least of all for a pink like me.~

~If I told Daddy, he wouldn't let anyone take you away.~

The girl obviously had some sort of misconception about who ran the household here, Marne thought, but he kept that observation from her curious mind. ~Does it hurt when they yell? I mean, you cover your shoulders.~

~Sort of. I don't really, *really* hurt unless you grab me too hard or it's really hot or really cold. I can *feel* them yelling, though, and it's not comfy. Is that why you don't like hugging? It hurts?~

He turned. Kyra's tricolored human eyes were half-closed, and her breathing was slowing; she was tired. He didn't know much about humans except they needed more rest than those of his race. ~It doesn't hurt. We just don't.~

~Oh.~

Marne looked around for a place for himself. His cage was on the other side of the room, and he wanted nothing to do with it, though the adults had thought he would sleep there...like a dog. He glared through the crack in the door.

~There's room here. I can roll over; I won't touch you.~

Marne startled and looked at her.

~You said you didn't know where to sleep, and you were angry at them for thinking you were a dog.~

~I didn't...say...~ He hadn't covered his thoughts, though. This one was different indeed. Where she slept looked comfortable enough. After glancing up, he grabbed the edge of the mattress, wedged his foot on the step of wood, and jumped up beside Kyra. As promised, she rolled away from him. Feeling nervous, he burrowed under the blankets as she had and lay there. Not yet ready to sleep, he began to practice guarding his thoughts better.

Nicolas had more pull than Marne had given him credit for, and the alien settled into life with the Starbard family. His role, as the girl's father had explained, was to be Kyra's tutor, with the main goal of helping her learn to speak by using their telepathic connection. Nicolas also clearly had a better idea of what a Naratsset was and what one could do than Marne had initially thought.

Zalana ignored the Naratsset or treated him like a dog anyway, but he stayed. He didn't eat at the table, but Kyra refused to let him eat off the floor, so he was given food in Kyra's bedroom. She'd offered to put down a blanket and a place setting for him, like a picnic, but Marne wanted no part in that. In his last home, one of the little girls had done that, insisting he wear her dolls' clothes, and he would not endure that again.

The baby, Alyce, found him amusing and often reached for his antennae, and Kyra would get scolded for scolding the baby. Sometimes Kyra would just scowl, while at other times she tried to argue that his antennae were just as sensitive as her shoulders. Arguing with Zalana, however, was useless.

Until Kyra finally spoke her argument.

"Thahht...hohrts...heem!"

Marne had become used to the slur in her voice; she couldn't hear what she was saying. Zalana stared at her daughter, mouth open and voiceless, as though Kyra had taken the woman's speech.

"Eet horts...laike–laike mahi nick ahund shooldahrs," Kyra stated.

"I…see…" the woman managed, looking uneasily between the Naratsset and Kyra. She scooped up Alyce, who giggled at the noise her sister had made, and quickly walked out of the room.

Marne felt his friend's flying and plummeting emotions viscerally. She was thrilled her mother had heard her, but Zalana's reaction… He vocalized it for her, in her mind and aloud: "All those years she's wanted to hear you, and it's just *that*! 'I…see…?'"

Kyra shook her head at him and anxiously looked around the corner toward the kitchen. He knew she could sense when he spoke both verbally and mentally; she'd told him it felt different. He looked at her. "Well, if she wasn't listening to you!" he said, crossing his arms, partly wishing the woman was listening from the kitchen and comprehended how much her eldest daughter wanted to be heard.

~Can you ever not read my mind?~ she asked. ~*You* keep *me* out sometimes.~

Marne hesitated, considering. ~You don't know how to keep me out? You do it sometimes, you know.~

~No, I don't know.~

He sat down across from her and pondered further. Teaching her to speak aloud had taken up so much time and was tiring for him; he'd taken for granted that she was gleaning the telepathy. He wasn't sure where to begin with that. ~Think…of a wall…between your thoughts and mine.~ The girl did so and he winced. ~Like that but… you don't need to do it so ha——~

She cut off his instructions as she leaped to her feet, and then she ran toward the door, squealing one of the four words she'd insisted Marne teach her to say perfectly: "Daddy!"

Another thing that surprised him—despite not being able to hear, Kyra always seemed to know when someone was approaching the house. It took her longer to perceive the person if they were on foot, as Nicolas traveled, but she seemed able to detect that a coach was driving up the Starbard house's half-hidden gravel road long before even Marne could hear it.

"Hey, baby girl!" Her father beamed at her, gathering her into a big hug as he walked through the door. Marne scootched back and watched. He could feel their affection for each other from this distance. Remembering it helped him keep his patience when Kyra struggled for the millionth time over a particular sound she couldn't master. The girl should have begun speech earlier; he felt her brain fighting to make connections it had outgrown and forgotten.

"I love you, Daddy!" All of the words she'd insisted that she had to say perfectly. Thrilled as he always was, Nicolas showered her with kisses. The physicality of these people, this family in particular, still bothered Marne.

He heard Zalana coming and moved farther away, leaning into the material of the sofa and knowing that its creamy white did nothing to disguise his bright coloring. No matter—she still disregarded him and kissed her husband. Marne wished Kyra would come back, but she still held her father's hand.

"Isn't Kyra doing well with talking?" Nic said excitedly. "Tell your mom you love her, sweetie!"

"I love you, Mauwm." She hadn't practiced that so much.

The woman smiled but cringed. Marne clenched his hands into fists, but a sharp look from Nicolas kept him silent. In addition to underestimating the control her father wielded in the house, Marne had also not realized that some of Kyra's psychic gifts came from him, though the man seemed mostly unaware of his abilities. Nor was he anywhere near as strong as his daughter. Only on occasions like this did the Naratsset know the adult human could sense his thoughts.

"Can you get time off in two weeks?" Zalana asked.

"Maybe. Why?"

"I was called for a foretelling on Caterbree, and they are willing to make arrangements for the whole family."

"All of us?" he exclaimed, then paused. Lowering his voice and hardly moving his lips, he added, "Are you sure we should travel? After that UFC attack on that IGT Cruise…"

"Of course we should travel, Nic—" Zalana said, gesturing as if to wave away his worries.

Nicolas shook his head and spoke softly through a hardly-moving mouth. "Z, you *know* their stance on 'mystics'—"

"Starbards are a recognized and protected family line. Our vocation is considered sacred even among the secularists." Zalana raised her chin proudly. "Our presence on a ship or planet brings honor, and they wouldn't want anything happening to one of us." Kyra stared at her mother like one might stare at a queen, though Marne could tell she still had a hard time reading the woman's lips. Nicolas, on the other hand, only appeared more concerned. Zalana was undeterred by her husband's expression. "Besides, it was an isolated incident four months ago, between the two solar systems, and no one was hurt. The IGT security had it all under control, and security has been stepped up significantly." She cut a glare at Marne, so nasty that he cringed. Matching Nic's earlier lowered voice and fixed lips—clearly, this was something they didn't want Kyra to pick up on—she added, "And besides, we need the money I'll get for a foretelling like this." Bringing her voice back to its normal level, she continued. "And we need a vacation. You, Me, Kyra, and Alyce all together."

"An-dh Murh-nuh?" Kyra hadn't practiced his name that much, either. She looked at him with concern. Kyra knew how her mother felt about him, and Marne knew Kyra understood more about the family's money problems than her parents realized.

"Just the four of us," her mother stated. Kyra looked between her mother and Marne, then up at her dad. His lips were tight, and he gave Kyra a look that said he didn't want to fight.

"We cannot just leave him here!" she signed as soon as her mother headed for the kitchen.

"Kyra…let's talk about this later," her father said. "I'm hungry, aren't you?"

The girl scowled and folded her arms. Nicolas gave her a stern look and, taking her upper arms, steered her around and toward the dining room. In a couple of minutes, Kyra, still frowning, ran out with a bowl and utensils for Marne.

~I'm not leaving without you! I'll stay here by myself!~ she declared with enough passion to make the Naratsett shake his head. ~Sorry,~ she added, seeing his reaction and lowering her projected emotion.

Marne took his bowl and shook his head. ~Don't fight with them. I'll be fine…just leave me some food.~

~No!~

He looked up and blinked. ~You *want* me to starve?~

~No! I mean…you have to come with us!~

~No, I don't.~ He headed toward her room, knowing better than to eat in the sitting room, much less near the perfectly creamy furniture. ~You got along fine for ten years without me. You'll be fine for this trip. Your mother thinks you're depending on me too much. That's what she was saying before.~

~But you're my friend! I can't leave you behind! What if something happens to you? What if you run out of food? And who will get water slips for you? Or—~

~I will be fine. I lived alone before…before I was captured. I can live alone while you're gone.~

Kyra's lips trembled as she sensed his emotion. He put up his own wall against her thoughts.

~How…how did you get captured?~

~I don't want to talk about it.~

~But—~

Marne tilted his antennae toward the kitchen as he heard Nicolas call, "Kyra!"

"What's the point, Nicolas? She still can't hear!" He just barely kept himself from cringing at Zalana's tone.

"But Marne can." He did roll his eyes at that, another trick he'd picked up from humans…one he rather liked, because with his solid-colored eyes, they couldn't tell when he did it.

"I wish you'd stop referring to that *thing* as a person!"

"Z, please!"

~They want you in the dining room, and they're getting angry,~ Marne told her, and turned toward the stairs that led up to the bedrooms.

He felt Kyra pause to watch him go before she ran to the dining room. Even halfway up the stairs, Marne felt her discomfort when she returned to what he supposed were sharp looks from both her parents.

She didn't realize how lucky she was, though. Despite his dislike of Zalana and her apparent issues with her eldest daughter, Marne knew that both Kyra's parents loved her.

"Caterbree is against slavery of any sort!"

"You hardly refer to him as a person—"

"That's not the point, Nicolas!"

They continued. At least Kyra didn't ask him to translate this time, but Marne knew she wasn't asleep. She couldn't sleep when they argued; the noise, the vibrations, or something affected her. He still wasn't sure how it worked, but he had noticed Zalana had exceptionally sensitive skin, too, though not as sensitive as Kyra's. He agreed with Nicolas that it had to be tied to the Starbard gene, which both daughters had. He wondered how the baby ever slept.

Maybe it was enough that the baby knew she wasn't the one being yelled about.

That hadn't been his thought. At night, when she was falling asleep, Kyra slipped in and out of his mind...unless he consciously kept her out.

He put up a barrier, and she felt it. Her breath tickled the back of his head as she sighed. He had become accustomed to her nearness at night, even when she would put an arm across him in her sleep. It was how humans showed affection, he understood, though until he met Kyra, he'd never experienced an affectionate touch. Humans were very tactile; he'd just normally been on the painful side of such communication. He figured it made up for their lack of psychic abilities. Besides, he appreciated her restraint when she was not sleeping; he sensed that she wanted to hug him, or even kiss him, at times, when she accomplished something. He tried to keep from cringing at those thoughts.

"If the Caterbreians can realize he's a sentient being, why can't you? Right now, he's the only friend that Kyra has!"

"Kyra should make more friends—"

"Where? She can't go to a decent school on this planet!"

"The schools aren't prepared to deal with—with..."

"With anyone who isn't perfectly coded?" Nicolas exploded. "It's insane! Back home, we had schools for the deaf, for the blind; everyone was welcome!"

"Everyone *is* welcome on Cordelier—"

"To an extent. People like Kyra are 'welcome' in specific schools that prepare them for mindless jobs where no 'normal' person has to interact with them—"

"Nicolas! It's not like that, not like how you're saying it! You make it sound awful! People like Kyra are protected, safe—"

"Protected from what? Living normal lives?"

"*Normal?* Nic, *we* don't have a normal life! We're Starbards. You knew that when you married me, when… when you came back here with me to find my family. You knew the life we were coming to."

"I did, and I wouldn't change that for anything. You *know* this. I love you, and I love the girls. I just wish…"

"Wish what? What do you wish, Nic?"

"That…that you'd just give Kyra more of a chance—"

"More of a chance? What *exactly* do you mean, Nic? I love her! I just don't know what to do with her sometimes."

"And nothing I do works for you? Did she not just say 'I love you' this evening? Thanks to Marne being able to train her to speak better than either of us can teach her?"

"Nicolas, stop, please…just stop a minute."

Marne hardly heard the last bit. Their voices had softened, and Kyra's breathing began to slow as she fell asleep. He wondered what they were saying, but even more, he wondered what Kyra was feeling that he couldn't pick up. She said she sensed things in her hands and shoulders, but Marne felt his antennae should have picked up whatever cue allowed Kyra some peace. It was more than emotions; he couldn't feel the emotions from one floor up, not even as strongly as they ran during fights. Even if her empathic abilities were better than his, which they could be, he'd have sensed what she sensed. No, something else outside of his abilities affected her. He'd find out. She needed sleep, and she didn't need to hurt so much.

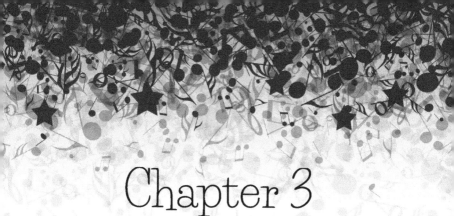

Chapter 3
Time, Space, and Affection

21 NIVOSE 897

I can't get my parents to take Marne, too. I've failed. I don't know what to do, what if something happens to him? He's much smaller than me. Can he even reach the refrigerator or the faucet? Dad's talking to him now, but he said I had to pack. In other words, I'm not supposed to know what they're talking about. I wonder if Marne will tell me what they say. He probably won't. He usually does what Daddy says. I wonder how old he is? He is older than me, I'm sure. He's a lot smarter than me.

Will he let me hug him, just this once? We're going to be gone almost three months with the travel, or more, really, because of the time thing that Dad tried to explain to me...but it could be almost a year on Cordelier, depending on "orbit!" When I was really little, Daddy told me Mom was gone almost two years when she visited Tulaine, which is in another solar system. I'm going to miss Marne so much! And he'll be alone for so long! I know he's only been here for about four months, but I love him! He's my best friend! I don't want to go to Caterbree.

Mom thinks I should be excited because I've never left the planet before. Maybe Marne's not upset because he doesn't want to go in a starship again. It must have been horrible when he was in his cage, but he won't talk about his home or what happened after he was captured. He puts up his wall-thing in his mind. It must hurt a lot. Maybe if he wasn't afraid of hugs he'd find they help. I always feel better when Daddy hugs me…especially after I feel them fighting. He tells me it will be fine and he gives me a hug and kisses.

Maybe Marne doesn't like thinking about his home because they don't hug so nothing ever gets better. I wonder what his parents were like or if he had any sisters or brothers and what his planet looks like. I hope they have diaries on Caterbree because I might need a new one. I will write everything down so I can tell him, and maybe practice drawing. Dad won't be at work, so he can show me more, and it's vacation, sort of.

I wish Marne could see a foretelling by Mom. Maybe he'd like her more. He gets angrier at her than I do…but if he knew what it was like to sing to the stars, then maybe he'd understand. She wishes I could because it's such a beautiful thing, to sing and glow like that… and tell the stories of what's going to happen and have everyone cry and hold you and take care of you. I'm sad that I can't, and so is she, but she probably doesn't know that she's sad about it. She likes to look like she has everything under control. Marne doesn't understand that, either.

I'll have to draw a picture with Mom and the stars. I'll have Daddy help me so it's perfect. And then I'll make a frame and we can put it on the wall and it will be like being there again. I think Marne will like the pictures I draw and the stories about traveling in a starship when you're not in a cage.

I still wish he could go.

~What's wrong with you? Are you sick?~

"Huh?" Kyra murmured, wiping her sleeve across her eyes. She'd been trying to talk more around Marne so he'd help her fix her speech.

~That. What you just did! What's wrong with your eyes? Can you see all right?~

"Huh? Yuh." She paused, then realized what he was talking about. She opened her mouth and then decided it was too complicated to say yet. ~I'm crying. I'm sad that you have to stay here, and I'll miss you, and I'm worried about if you can get to the food and the water…and what if someone breaks in and hurts you?~

~I will be fine. I promise. I told you, I've lived alone before.~

~In a world where everyone was bigger than you?~

Marne paused. ~No, but it was even harder. I can climb things and move some things with my mind, if I have to. Nothing big…~

~You can move things with your mind?~

~You've seen me.~

Kyra thought a moment, then shook her head. Marne tilted his head in thought. ~The first night I was here and you tried to hug me. I made you move.~

~You shocked me, like electricity.~

~Well, you are a lot bigger than me. I couldn't actually move *you*.~

Kyra frowned at him, hurt. ~I didn't know you could move things with your mind…or…well, I guess I don't know much of anything about you!~ Her thoughts returned to the journal she'd just packed, remembering all the things she'd written.

His slit-like mouth fluttered with a sigh, and she realized she wasn't keeping her thoughts to herself.

She pouted. ~See, I don't know any of that, and I can't remember to shut you out and you shut me out all the time!~

~I don't shut you out all the time.~

~Whenever it's about you.~

~None of it's happy. You don't need to know it. You're going away, and you should have fun. Your dad will be around, and he can teach you anything I can, now.~

Her eyes welled up again as he changed the subject and ignored her argument. She folded her arms stubbornly and looked him in the eyes. ~Can I get things like you can?~ she challenged, picturing her hands reaching into his head.

"Stop!" He backed away, letting her feel that she'd hurt him. ~I never did that to you!~

~But you get stuff I don't want you to get all the time.~

~*Not* all of the time! Only when you don't realize you're sending it.~

Kyra swallowed hard, blinked back more tears, and got up to check her suitcases. Behind her, he paced. As small as he was, she felt his walking back and forth.

~Do you really want to know about me?~

She didn't answer, letting him read whatever thoughts crossed her mind. Moving a few things around in her suitcase, she shut it hard and then began rearranging her toy shelf. She didn't play with her toys as often as she used to; mostly, she spent her time trying to learn more. Especially now, when she had Marne to help her. She liked spending time with him more than any doll or game she used to play with by herself.

~One minute.~

She felt his footsteps as he left the room and came back, turning quickly enough to see the door shut and lock.

~Yes, I just did that with my mind. Your mother already hates me.~

~She doesn't *hate* you,~ Kyra managed, amazed at seeing her door seemingly act on its own.

~I know I don't have to ask…but I do, for this. Do you trust me?~

Kyra looked at him. As smooth as his face was, she had learned to read it somewhat, or perhaps it was just that she had become more attuned to his emotions. He seemed almost scared. ~Of course I trust you.~

~I'll show you what happened, but I told you, it's not happy. Also, you won't need to worry about me while you're gone. You'll know I'll be all right. Sit down.~

She did as she was told, leaning against the side of her bed.

~Now, don't be scared.~

The warning didn't work. Kyra gasped in horror as six spindly, insect-like legs, black in contrast to his pink body, sprouted from his neck and pointed toward her.

~I said——~

~You could have warned me you had…things!~

~You saw them on the other ones at the market.~

~Not that big! Not pointed at me!~

He pulled them back away from her. ~If they knew I still had mine, they would have broken them…like the ones you saw. They were broken.~

"Oh," she both said and thought as she stared at the long appendages. ~What are you going to do with them?~

~Touch your face, go into it, where nerves to your brain are close to the skin.~

~*You are going to burrow into my skin?!*~

Marne winced and retracted his leggy-things once more, folding the appendages slowly.

Kyra bit her lip, realizing her reaction had distressed him a lot. ~Wait! Go ahead…will it…hurt?~

"You've got...things?!"

~I don't know.~ He still shied away from her. ~It doesn't hurt *us*. It's…it's how we show affection to each other…in a manner…but I don't know if it will cause you pain.~

Kyra took a deep breath. ~Well…go ahead.~

~Are you sure?~

She nodded.

~What if it does hurt you? I didn't think…~

~I'll tell you if it does. It will probably sting at first, like a doctor's shot. Humans feel a lot through our skin.~ She tried to sound knowledgeable about those sort of things. She knew enough about doctors and shots, in any case.

Marne nodded and moved his…things…closer. Then paused. ~They're called *kaatsin*.~

Kyra tried to repeat it. "Kah-aht-zeen."

~Very good! You actually say it better than most humans.~

His assurance and approval eased her shaking some, but she still felt some apprehension—though more excitement—that Marne was sharing some alien secret with her. As the six points drew nearer, she tried not to wince, but had to settle for closing her eyes.

They felt like fingernails or pencil points as they moved across her face. Two stopped at her hairline, directly above her eyebrows. Two others poked on either side of her eyes. The final two went around her face to where her neck met her skull.

It did hurt, for a minute, a pinprick and a little burning, but it immediately subsided and felt…pleasant. She blinked and found herself standing in a little village with smallish houses. Naratssets milled around her, not noticing her, which made sense because she was in one of Marne's memories. She walked around, but not for long. Pictures began to flood her mind. She felt Marne trying to slow them down, but his own mind jumbled them. She saw his parents, dark-blue, both of them, but couldn't tell which was his mother or father. They looked the same to her. And they were all talking in her head! All at once! It wasn't as jarring as when she'd first thought she'd "heard" Marne, but she knew the sensation now. She just had to sort out all the new "voices" and focus.

Then she saw Marne, tiny and pink and huddled in a corner. They were talking about him, and he knew it. Kyra started to understand what the others were saying.

The words were all too familiar: "Defect," "Not good enough," "How could this happen?" "Deformed." But then it got worse. "Market." "Dealers." "Can't keep him around long." One of them didn't want to sell him. Mother. Night came, and Mother lifted him in a kind of bubble held by her stick-like *kaatsin* (Kyra didn't think they'd be so strong; they looked like they would break with a little weight!) and carried him to the woods, leaving him there. Anything was better than the market.

More time passed. Food grew on trees, and he quickly learned what was good. He could make it come down from the trees if it wasn't too far up. He missed his family, didn't understand, and tried to go back. More blue Naratssets, constables, were already at his house.

"Heard you had a light?"

"He died, burned the body as prescribed."

"Then we can look around."

"Of course."

The constables weren't happy. Back to the woods, but sometimes returning, trying to find Mother. Mother had brought him to the woods, so surely she must wonder if he were all right.

Took a long time to find courage...and even longer for the constables to stop visiting. Mother didn't want him. She ignored him. He followed her back. They saw him, and he had to run away. They would hurt him.

Time passed in a swirl of color. Marne found a way to make himself look blue by rubbing a flower on his skin. He made it back home, but his family was no longer there. Everyone was gone, parents, siblings, eggs—they laid eggs? Kyra's thought pulled her away from being part of the memory, making things look fuzzy and blurred, and created a sensation like a string pulling out of her stomach, so she refocused on watching what was going on.

A main city, like hers, but smaller. More glass, less metal. Metal made powers harder to use. Glass and crystal. It was pretty. The Naratssets here could lift themselves up, move big things, such as a type of electrotram, with their minds. Move a whole planet if they had to…he listened to conversations, but he still had to hide. They could sense him, sense he was wrong. Kyra struggled to catch everything, but Marne's mind moved faster than hers, and he could comprehend almost all the conversations at once. The others would know he was weak if he tried to talk to any of them.

It was a jumble again. His mind didn't want to remember it all, so it mashed the memories together. The sensation almost buzzed in her head, so Kyra tried to shake it clear, forgetting he held it and finding she couldn't move it. A moment of panic came, but she felt Marne calm her down. She missed part of the story, and he wasn't about to tell it again. He was arrested, along with his family because somehow the other Naratssets could distinguish family bloodlines. His parents signed papers, because Marne was still a "child" and technically belonged to them, and they watched as he was loaded into a cage. The cage was taken on an electrotram, which they called a "train," and out into the country.

Humans were in the country, their starships nasty metal marks on otherwise beautiful, soft, yellow grasses. Humans were big, hairy, and smelly. There were other "lights" there, but none of them pink. The humans paid gems, jewels, and beautiful boxes to the blue Naratsset constables for the light-colored Naratssets. For slaves. From conversations, Marne knew his family's share of his price would now go to the capital city, since his mother had tried to hide him. After the trading, the humans loaded the now-enslaved Naratssets into cages and the cages into a dark starship.

~I don't know how long we were in there before our first stop… You don't want to know about that part,~ Marne interrupted the vision. The pictures faded to grey and colored mist in her head.

~Yes, I do.~

~I don't want to *remember* that part.~

~Okay…sorry.~

She felt the *kaatsin* move on her face and neck as he shook his head, and she made a face. The pleasant feeling, like the tingles she got whenever one of her parents brushed her hair, returned, and she simply saw a swirl of lights.

~There,~ he spoke again. ~You're stronger at the telepathy now. You know everything I know…and you'll know if anything happens to me, no matter where you are.~

It stung again when he removed the insect-leg things. He did it slowly, too, but explained that he had to heal the holes he'd made in her skin.

~Not bad,~ Marne thought to her. The edges of his mouth tightened in the best imitation of a smile he could make. She sensed he was projecting happiness at her, though she sensed more feelings, a lot of anger, sadness, and pain, from the memories.

Marne folded his *kaatsin* back up, and they slid down into his neck, like one of Mom's kitchen knives into its holder.

Kyra stood up and looked in the mirror on the whitewood dresser across from her bed. There were tiny pink dots in the six places. Her hair covered all but the ones next to her eyes. She sat back down and looked at Marne but didn't know what to say.

An understanding came to her. It didn't matter that she couldn't say anything. This understanding came from him, in the same manner that she could sense his happiness. It wasn't words, like when they mindspoke, but the communication seemed...deeper, more real.

~Yes, we can sense each other more,~ he explained. ~As if you were more like a Naratsset. And you can keep me out easier when you want to, too.~ He sounded and felt sadder now, and quite tired.

"Muhrn-nah," she tried to say, and stopped herself as she went to reach for him.

~You can give me a hug if you want to. It won't...bother me as much now.~ He offered a feeling of apology, too, for it being so hard for him to deal with her touching.

He had hardly finished this thought when she wrapped her arms around him and nestled her cheek against his head. Lightly, he patted her arm. ~Humans are too tactile,~ he commented, and she let him go. ~But I will miss you while you are gone, Kyra. And thank you for wanting to make sure I'm all right.~

She couldn't keep herself from embracing him again or kissing the side of his face. She felt him make a noise and released him once more, with an apology, which he waved away. She giggled and hefted her suitcases off the bed so they could sleep.

~And I don't think I'm much older than you, either, though I think humans age slower. It was one of the things you wanted to know before.~

~Really? Neat!~ She finished pulling down her covers. ~I'm going to draw you a picture of Mom singing with the stars... I wish you could see it.~

Marne cocked his head. ~I believe I'll see a starsinging someday...but I look forward to seeing your pictures.~

Kyra smiled and hopped into bed, waiting for him to follow, and wondering if he could turn off the light for her.

~Yes, I can get the light.~

She watched eagerly as the switch flipped off. Her giggles dissolved into a grin of awe as she watched him jump-float, in the nightlight's dim glow, and land with hardly a thump on her bed. She sensed that he liked making her happy, and shared an appreciation of his happiness, too, then scooted to one side so she wouldn't encroach on his space.

He didn't move at first, and she felt him thinking to himself. Biting her lip, she tried not to pry. She didn't have to wait long before he reached over and touched his hand to her face, as her Dad sometimes did, only with his much smaller hand.

He withdrew it quickly, but she knew he was trying to show affection on her level. ~Good night, Kyra. May your journey tomorrow be safe.~ He lay down and took his corner of the blankets.

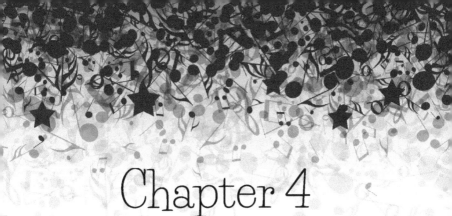

Chapter 4
Stars and Other Discoveries

25 Nivose 897

Snow today. Cold powder, Daddy calls it. He says Mom and I don't know what real snow is; it's never wet enough on Cordelier for "real" snow. All I know is it's cold and windy and I wore two quilted sweaters and my coat. Mom did too, and Alyce looked like a big bun of blankets with a red face that Mom put another blanket over, one made of yarn and little holes, so she could breathe. She's been walking for a while, but Mom put her in the carry thing so she could put on more blankets, I think.

The starship was much bigger than any of the ones we saw at the market. WAAAAAAAAYYY bigger, with big rooms for all of us—well, I'm sharing with Alyce. It also has three different places to eat, a place to swim, and a room with one full wall of screens that distributes snacks and stuff! It's bigger than the one at the supermarket!

Anyway, they're fighting again. Alyce is napping and I went into the room that joins our bedrooms, the one with the couches and the table, and I could feel them fighting. Daddy gave me a sharp look, and he held his mouth so his lips didn't move, but I know he was talking to Mom because hers were still moving a little. So, I took my journal and went for a walk. There's lots of people watching the wall-screens. Four different screens are streaming the eqcannus *racing and two of the screens are showing the messages about being alert and telling the guards—who are Everywhere!—if we see anything "unusual" or "suspicious." The message is printed out and scrolls through lots of different languages, so it was interesting at first, when I saw it on the other screens around the ship, because I could practice reading Saxonic, Formal, and Common Cordelieran, but then it got boring because it was the same message over and over and over again.*

Some of the eqcannuses *are very pretty, with blue and grey fur and black hooves. I wonder why gelatin isn't black? Do they make the blue stuff from blue hooves? I don't see any blue hooves, just black and brown and some white. I wonder what they look like in real life. When they're done running their race and walking with their owners back to the kennel-corrals, you can see that their heads come up almost to their owners' shoulders.*

I wonder if they can talk like Marne and people just don't listen. Would they want to run away? They never look happy, but I don't know if they just look that way or if it's because they are always shown after the race with the white spit coming out of their mouths and their thick tongues hanging over their sharp teeth. I wonder why their tongues don't get cut by their teeth. I think meeting one would be scary.

I wonder if Marne can talk to animals, too. I should ask him when we get back.

Kyra jumped and snapped shut her journal as a man sat down on the other side of her small round table. "Don't worry," he said slowly, seeming to wait for her to look at him before he spoke. "I won't read your diary. Do you mind if I sit here?"

Kyra's mind ran with all her parents' warnings about strangers and news stories that said terrorists could be anyone. She looked around, and there were lots of empty tables. Why had he picked hers? She looked in the direction of the door, where the two guards were stationed, then back to the man. Her mouth open, she contemplated getting a guard because this was "unusual" and maybe even "suspicious." Except this stranger looked very familiar.

"I'm sorry, perhaps this is quite rude of me. You did look busy. I can find another table; it's just that this one is my favorite. I like the pictures." He pointed at the table. Following his hand, Kyra noticed the different-colored pieces of wood that fit together to make a scene of a child cuddling with a lamb under a tree. She looked back at him, and he spoke. "I think they were going for Blake. A commendable attempt, though a far cry from his quality. Do you know William Blake?"

Kyra shook her head. The man, who had mostly white hair with some grey, pulled out a book from a brown shoulder bag by his side—he must have a lot of money to have a book so old and in that kind of leather and gold binding! Her parents only had a few like that, and those had all come with Dad, who'd snuck them off his home planet when he'd escaped with Mom. With a look to see that she was watching him, he began to recite:

Little Lamb who made thee
Dost thou know who made thee
Gave thee life & bid thee feed.
By the stream & o'er the mead;
Gave thee clothing of delight,
Softest clothing wooly bright...
"There's more. Do you like it?"

Kyra nodded, though it was more his expressions as he read that appealed to her than the many words she didn't know or couldn't understand, despite how clearly he formed them on his lips.

"Do you mind if I stay here, then? You may borrow the book." He smiled, making his eyes sparkle. They were blue, like her father's. He handed her the book, one finger holding it open to what he'd read. Her Dad had read her things like this, too—*poems, he'd called them.* When her Mom foretold, she wrote her visions in long, narrative poems.

She read the poem the man had just recited and a few others. Then she saw people jumping and moving in her peripheral vision. Putting the book down, she looked past them at the wall screens. One of the *eqcannuses* had fallen just in front of the finish line. The others trampled it.

Kyra felt her throat catch as she watched in horror as the injured *eqcannus* writhed on the ground. Blood pooled on the dirt track and foam covered most of its muzzle. She watched two people approach it, shake their heads, and throw the body into a hovercraft with a box on the back. When the cameras returned to the other animals, Kyra looked to her companion, who was shaking his head.

"Barbaric practice, if you ask me," he said. Again, she noticed he tilted his head so she could see his lips.

Kyra nodded. People began to sit down as the screens showed another race starting. The cameras focused on the hooves. She halfheartedly signed "gelatin."

"There's that, too." He nodded.

She only saw him speak out of the corner of her eye and looked back at him.

He winked and signed, "My father was deaf, so my whole family learned sign language."

She gaped in surprise and studied him again, carefully.

"So, aside from them being a source of gelatin, what else did you learn about the *eqcannuses*?" he asked.

Kyra shook her head and shrugged.

"Well, the saddest thing about them is that they're not meant to do anything but race. They were one of the first things scientists really played with genetics for, before Cordelier outlawed that much manipulation."

Kyra looked at him curiously, trying to understand what he said. Something on his face told her that this was important.

"You see, *eqcannuses* aren't natural things. The scientists engineered them. They took genes from thoroughbred horses and some from greyhounds and ended up with something that's too big to be a house pet, not strong enough for any draft work, and too vicious for either, anyway."

"The scientists build them?" She looked in confusion at the screens.

The man chuckled. "Not like they would build a bridge. They are created in laboratories rather than in nature. That kind of work is illegal now. The most they can do is therapy to correct health issues."

"Except me," she signed, frowning. "They cannot fix me."

"If they couldn't fix you, perhaps you really didn't need to be fixed."

"I'm deaf," she gestured emphatically.

The man shrugged. "Perhaps you are deaf because there is something so special about you that if you weren't deaf, your abilities would be too much for others to handle."

Kyra raised an eyebrow skeptically and huffed.

"I'm not the first to say that, am I? I bet you already know some things you do better than other people, right?"

The girl made a dismissive wave but found her mind winding around what the man said. Her dad had told her many times that she could fix things he took apart better than some of his coworkers, who spent years in school to get their jobs. And Marne kept saying he'd never met any human who'd taken so well to using telepathy. Her drifting thoughts came back when a pink drink was placed in front of her. "It's a Shirley Temple," the man said when she looked up. He lifted a brown drink of his own. "I figured you might like it."

Kyra looked at it for a few minutes. Cherries floated beneath the ice; she loved cherries. She glanced at him. He was still technically a stranger, and her parents would have a fit if they knew she were sitting with him, much less accepting food. What if he had put a poison in the drink and intended to kidnap her?

The older man quickly looked up and toward the entrance. Kyra snapped her head around to see her dad calling her name.

"Kyra!" Her father ran to her, red-faced and looking out of breath and scared, like he had when she'd wandered off among the Naratsset cages in the market "What do you think you're doing? Your mother and I have been looking all over for you."

Immediately, she bit her lip and stood up. She opened her mouth and held up her hands, but had no idea what to say. Her gaze returned to her older companion, who stared intently at her father with an expression she couldn't quite read. Nicolas turned to address the man. She didn't misread the look of shock on her Dad's face. "Dad?" he said.

She recognized that word, and her eyes grew wide.

"Well, son, isn't this a coincidence!"

"When did you leave— I mean…how? No one on Earth…"

"Well, my boy, if it were no one, how did *you* leave?" He smiled and winked at Kyra. "I've always known interesting people who could do interesting things. I saw pretty much everything I wanted to see on Earth and decided I wanted to see some new things. About fifteen years ago, give or take with the time dilation—you know how that goes—I took off, quite literally."

Her father's mouth moved but Kyra couldn't detect any words. The old man stood up and offered his hand. Nicolas pulled him into an embrace, tears filling his eyes. Smiling, the old man hugged him and patted his back.

"You've been on Cordelier? And we haven't seen each other? Did you know? I mean..."

"Did I know you were on Cordelier? I saw your picture a few times with your lovely wife, when she did the foretelling a little over a year ago, but I've been trying to get off the planet for a while. I figured we'd said our goodbyes in Manchester; why do it again? But today I happened to see one of the loveliest Pembroke noses I have ever seen, and I had a feeling that God was telling me something."

Nicolas looked around nervously.

His father huffed. "The Jacobins would all roll over in their graves. The planet takes their calendar and a good portion of their social structure and turns it into an agnostic mandate—and actually enforces it planetwide, while the originators couldn't even keep France in line."

Kyra watched the conversation, reading her grandfather's lips clearly but still not understanding most of it. Her mind was still wrapped around the fact that she had been talking to her dad's dad. She had never met a grandparent before. And to learn that *his* dad had been deaf like she was!

"...we are being quite rude, Nic, and my granddaughter looks as lost as she is excited." The old man squatted before her, signing as he spoke. "I have a confession to make, Kyra, and I hope you'll forgive me. I recognized you because you are almost the spitting image of my wife, Magdalena, your grandmother, when she was a wee one."

Feeling her father speak, she turned back to him. "...got her mom's eyes, though." Nicolas sat and pulled Kyra onto his lap, and she adjusted herself so she could see both men's mouths. "Starbard eyes." He kissed her cheek as he pulled out his tablet and tapped out a message to her mother, assuring Zalana he'd found Kyra and all was well

"Ah, the next great foreteller?" The old man smiled, returning to his seat.

Kyra felt heat rise to her cheeks. Mom had made it clear that a proper Starbard ought to be able to hear. Her father disagreed. His cheek, rough from needing a shave, nodded against her and he hugged her proudly.

"I knew you were something special, Kyra," the old man said, lifting his glass of brown liquid in a salute.

The girl shrugged and reached for her own drink. Satisfied this man was no longer a stranger, she eagerly drank and fished for cherries as the two men spoke over her head. Instead of trying to read their lips, she focused on the feel of their voices; her grandfather's voice *felt* different as it brushed her left side. It was an interesting sensation that she hadn't explored before, so she closed her eyes and concentrated on *just* the feel of each voice. They also laughed a lot, and that made her happy. Whenever people laughed, it sent pleasant tingles over her shoulders and hands.

After a while, she grew tired. Shifting to get comfortable, she snuggled closer to her dad's chest. She felt him lift his left hand and figured he was checking his watch. He shook her to wake her up. "Say good night to your granddad, sweetie," he said.

Granddad was a new word for her, and she wasn't ready to "say" it yet, so she settled on just trying to say, "Good naite." The older man smiled and reached for a hug, which she eagerly gave. "Are you going to Caterbree, too?" she signed.

"Well, that's the next stop the ship's making, but I'm not staying there like you are," he explained. Her face fell in disappointment. "It's currently a three-week journey to Caterbree with the orbits this close, though, so we can spend some time together on the ship. If you'd like?"

Kyra nodded and reached for another hug, kissing the man on the cheek before her father led her back to their quarters to tuck her in. Although tired, it took her some time to fall asleep; she'd gotten used to the feel of Marne beside her, and the almost-humming feeling in her brain when they were near each other.

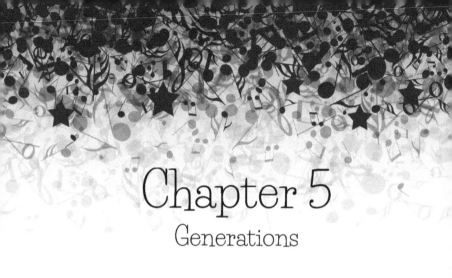

Chapter 5
Generations

Kyra sat by the pool, half-asleep, in one of the big long chairs that she only half-filled. To her left sat her dad, filling up a good portion of the chair, and to her right was her granddad, who took up slightly less chair. Her mother and Alyce had gone somewhere else; Mom said that too much light wasn't good for the baby and suggested the same for her older daughter.

Kyra had no intention or desire to leave, though. The room with the pool had lights that were bright and warm like the sun. The water was warm, too. She'd only gone swimming once before, and that was a colder area more south of the capital city of Napoleon, where her family lived. The water was so cold there it had hurt her hands, feet, and shoulders, so much that she'd clung to her dad and cried until he took her out. She remembered screaming as other bathers watched.

Nicolas was telling that very story to her granddad, who listened intently. They spoke in the conversational language that her father knew best, not the Common Cordelieran her mom used more. As she watched them talk, she realized why she sometimes had such a hard time reading her mother's lips. Even though her dad had spent more time teaching Kyra Common Cordelieran—well, he spent more time teaching Kyra *all* the languages she knew—his mouth moved differently than her mother's. Eyes half-closed behind dark glasses too big for her face, Kyra lazily watched her dad's lips as he recounted the swimming tale to Gerard, which was what her mother had called her grandfather last night, after her dad excitedly told her that Kyra's granddad was on the ship.

"...Kyra's hypersensitive to things, and bloody strong, too! I swear she was going to strangle me with those tiny arms of hers. I waded as fast as I could out of that mountain stream, around every other family trying to swim that summer, against a current swirling like Hell..."

She'd "heard" the story a thousand times before, so she picked up the book of poetry her grandfather had lent her. In the back were pictures, and she'd been looking at two of them in particular fascination. The print within the illustrations was too small for her to make out properly, but the pictures were listed beside the matching poems, which were printed in larger letters. She held the book open to the poem's page; she'd read it three times already.

Father! father! where are you going?
O do not walk so fast.
Speak, father, speak to your little boy
Or else I shall be lost.'
The night was dark, no father was there;
The child was wet with dew;
The mire was deep, and the child did weep,
And away the vapour flew.

The picture for that poem was all black except for the person in the middle, who looked more like a girl to Kyra than a boy, anyway. He was in an unbelted robe or dress. The poem was called "The Little Boy Lost." There was another poem about a little girl lost, but it was much longer and the picture didn't catch her attention. She wondered what had happened to the little boy's dad. Why would a dad leave like that? She could picture her mother doing that…especially if Kyra called out to her and she didn't want to hear how badly she spoke, but Daddy would always find her. There were still several words she didn't know the meaning of, and she wanted to ask what they meant, but her dad and her granddad were still talking to each other and laughing a lot.

Feeling the men speak and the warm heat on her, she began to fall asleep. She decided that sleeping was a good idea so she could stay up later that night and copy down some of the poems and pictures in her journal before going to bed. Maybe she could just change "boy" to "girl." Then again, she didn't really ever want to be lost.

"Oh, Nicolas! Look at her!"

Kyra was trying very hard not to cry, but every inch of her arms and legs—worse, her shoulders, neck, and face—felt as though she were on fire. She walked carefully, not wanting to let any part of her touch any other part. She looked at her parents, wondering what had happened.

"I'm sorry! I wasn't thinking…we haven't been in that kind of sun for how long? And she didn't say anything!"

"Go to the concierge and ask for this." Zalana wrote down something on paper. "As for you, my heart, a cool sponge bath will help. Come with me!"

Kyra glanced at her dad, who obediently left the suite. Her mother marched her to the bathroom and bade her strip and sit in the washtub. It had been years since she'd taken a bath. She usually used the disinfectant showers like everyone else, especially when water prices were high.

Her mother wet a cloth with cool water and lightly began to pat her daughter's arms, legs, shoulders, back, face—everywhere that her bathing suit hadn't covered. As she did so, they both relaxed. Kyra felt something from her mom, but Zalana's lips weren't moving. She stared for several minutes until her mother asked, "What?" She moved her lips deliberately and watched Kyra expectantly.

The girl shook her head. Zalana didn't know as many signs as Nicolas; Kyra couldn't explain what she'd felt coming from her mother. Sighing, she closed her eyes. She felt the sensation stronger this time and looked over again.

"You look like a raccoon," her mother smiled. "The light didn't get through your glasses." She traced the circles around Kyra's eyes, paused, and reached over to kiss her head. "I said not to stay out there long. I know you were looking at me when I said it. I made sure of it."

Kyra shrugged again.

"Well, I suppose it *is* a big thing to meet one of your grandparents. My mom and dad died before you were born."

Kyra watched her mother carefully, waiting for more information, but none came. Tensing her lips, she tried, "Wout heppend?"

Zalana started and stared at Kyra for a long time. After several minutes, the girl swallowed in embarrassment and looked down at the smooth white of the tub. She felt her mom breathe in a sigh and then her fingers pulled on her chin, drawing Kyra's face back up.

"There are some people who don't like Starbards," she explained. Kyra noted how slowly she spoke and paid close attention. "Some think we are undermining their beliefs, if they believe in a god or gods. Others think that we are mystics who don't fit into a scientific universe. My dad was a Starbard, like me." She paused, bit her lip, and added, "Like you and like Alyce. He and my mom had gone to a foretelling together and people attacked their ship and... and everyone died. Everyone..."

Her mother looked away, and Kyra saw tears in her eyes. She reached over and wiped her mom's lashes, thinking of the news reports from the attack months ago and all the security message screens. Zalana pulled away and wiped her own eyes, catching her daughter's hand and kissing it. "I'm sorry, but life isn't easy. There are people who want to hurt you for being a foreteller. There are bad people out there who'll take advantage of you. Hurt you. You know how your Dad and I always say not to talk to strangers? Those people are the reason why. Do you understand me?"

Kyra nodded emphatically. "Laike...laike the Yoo Eff See?" she asked. She'd gotten some information from Marne about a few of her parent's arguments about the UFC. And from when she insisted Marne tell her all the stuff they'd said when Mom had first announced they were going to Caterbree.

Zalana's eyes narrowed. "Who told you about the UFC?"

Kyra pressed her lips together. She didn't want to make her mother dislike Marne even more, so she didn't want to tell on him. Her eyes fell on the small wall-screen in front of the toilet and she pointed to it. "Noos. Casts. Ai ken read the scrohllz."

Her mother twisted her face in an expression Kyra couldn't quite read but made her shudder. She explained, "The Planetary Alliance has them under control. They're a tiny faction of people with very strict rules and beliefs... but, yes, they don't like Starbards. They tell people that we fake our abilities to get money. They would very much like us not to exist at all. If one of them tries to talk to you, find me, Dad, a guard, or some adult you can trust. Do you understand?"

Her mother had started speaking quickly again and the words hit her already-sore skin hard. Not exactly like yelling, but similar. Kyra understood most of it, though, and nodded quickly.

"Good. Your dad and I love you a lot, even though we get angry sometimes...you know that, right, Kyra?"

She nodded again, and her mother went back to patting the bright red skin with the cool cloth. After a few moments, she saw her mother's head turn. "That's your dad; he's back. Here, I got all the parts you can't reach. Pat all the rest and go to your room. I'll meet you there, okay?"

She bobbed her head up and down once again.

Zalana smiled. "You learn fast. Your dad only started teaching you to read lips, what, the beginning of the year?"

Once more, up and down she nodded.

"Good girl." She bent down and kissed Kyra's head. "I'll meet you in your room."

Zalana was up and out so Kyra didn't have to shake her head any more. She finished patting all the parts that hurt. Wrapping a towel around herself, she carefully walked toward her room, where her mother was waiting.

Zalana had a bottle in her hands. Taking off the towel, she carefully spread cool gel across the burns. Even with the lightest pressure, though, Kyra winced when her mother touched her shoulders and neck. She smiled sympathetically at her daughter. "It's meant to heal, sweetie; I'm sorry, but I have to."

Kyra didn't feel like nodding again, so she made a noise in her throat that she hoped sounded like agreement. Zalana nodded this time and finished applying the lotion.

"We should let it dry before you crawl into bed," her mother said, twisting the bottle closed. "It's so strange seeing Gerard again, you know?" Kyra shook her head. "I suppose not, no. I can't imagine meeting a grandparent for the first time in this kind of setting...just for a moment, really." Zalana sighed. "Make the most of it, Kyra. I can't begin to tell you how important it is."

"Ah weel," Kyra said, reaching her arms up as best as she could while her mom carefully pulled a soft nightgown over her head.

"When your dad took me to meet his parents, on his home planet, I was terribly scared," she told Kyra. "I was an alien to them, after all, more or less. I mean, we're both human, but I'd never been on his planet before, and I still wasn't getting their language right. Your dad actually learned Common Cordelieran much easier than I learned his language—and it seems Gerard has learned it pretty well, too.

"Anyway, there I was in a dress I thought was far too short, but it was the fashion, going on a terrestrial flyer with just your dad, a bunch of strangers, and no room to move, and his parents were going to pick us up—and I just looked terrible, and I felt like I was talking all wrong, and the first thing Gerard does is grab me in his arms, give me a big hug and two kisses, and say—in a language I understood better and that sounded a little like Common Cordelieran—'Well, we finally get to meet the angel Nicolas has been writing home about every day, two or three times a day even. And he hardly did you justice.'

"I was totally shocked, and then his mom came up, and you look an awful lot like her, and she also hugged and kissed me. She was just this delicate thing, though, and she spoke Nic's main language best, but that was all right. I could see everything she meant in her eyes, which were this crystal blue, a little lighter than your Dad's. I hugged her back but had to be careful. You see, she was sick, but she kept it hidden. I liked her immediately, though, and found all sorts of ways to help her around the house—but like a game so it didn't look like I was helping. She didn't want to look sick, after all." Zalana stopped speaking for a moment, sighed, and dabbed her eyes with her sleeve.

"They were everything I loved about your Dad. I had no one on his planet. I mean, you know how I crashed there, my heart. I was the only survivor. Worse, I didn't recognize any of the stars! And then your dad made me feel at home, safe. And that's just what his parents did, too. I felt like I had a family. After your dad graduated school—he was in school when I met him—we moved in with them, and I helped take care of his mother while he and his dad went to work. Then your dad asked me to marry him, and I knew Maggie—that was his mom, he called her 'Mum'—would want to see our wedding before she died. But I already knew I wanted to spend all my life with him, even if I was stuck on his planet. So we had a wedding ceremony at *his* grandparents' house, and you see those pictures every year, remember?"

"Mmn-hmn!" Kyra nodded, struggling with how wide she wanted to smile and how it hurt to stretch her cheeks. She'd gotten pieces of Mom's adventures on her dad's planet every year on their wedding anniversary, and every time there were different details. She loved discovering them all and finding out more. "An' then Daddy had to 'scape yoo from planet," she probed, wanting to hear her favorite part of the adventures.

"Another time, dear heart." Her mother kissed the top of her head gently. "But the lotion's dry, you're in your nightgown, and the best thing you can do is sleep, for your skin to heal. Okay?"

Kyra sighed heavily and tried to pout, but that hurt her burned cheeks, too. Nevertheless, she still wanted to hear the story. "Pleeze, Mauwm?" She paused, thinking of the story and how her dad called his mother "Mum," which looked easier to imitate. "Pleeze, Muhm?"

Her mother's mouth frowned, but there was a twinkle in her eyes that let Kyra know she wasn't unhappy.

"Preh-ty pleeze?"

The corner of Zalana's mouth curled up. "Do you promise to go right to sleep when I'm done?"

"Yu-es! Prom. Miss!"

With slightly more of a smile but one that also seemed to dim her eyes, Kyra's mother adjusted the covers and sat back down on the bed. "You know how I mentioned earlier that my parents were attacked by people who thought… who thought Starbards were doing something wrong and shouldn't exist? Like the UFC do? Well, there are people like that *all* over, and there are also people who want to be the only ones who get to hear Starbards. When we were on your father's home planet, there was a small group of humans; no one knew what they called themselves, if anything, but your dad once called them the 'Unnamed Ones,' and that stuck. They wanted me. They wanted to capture me and have me read only for them. I'd have been kept like a prisoner, a slave.

"Your dad and I had avoided them and stayed hidden for almost a year when another group of people, the kind that track and kill Starbards, arrived on the planet. They could make themselves look human—at least, that's the only way I saw them—and actually wanted to take over your dad's planet. They just called themselves 'The People.'

"The thing is, on your dad's planet, which he calls 'Earth,' most of the people in charge didn't want anyone else to know there actually *was* life on other planets, so they were trying to catch me while also trying to conceal and destroy both the Unnamed Ones *and* the People. All of this they were trying to do in secret. It's very hard to keep secrets, though, when one group, like the People, doesn't want to be kept a secret.

"One day, and this was about a month after your dad's mother passed away from her illness, I was alone in our house when the Unnamed Ones came for me. It was my own fault. Maggie, your dad's mom, had never heard me starsing, and it was the one thing she wanted to see before she passed. So I sang for her before she passed."

Zalana closed her eyes and took a deep breath, as if picturing the whole scene in her head. Kyra touched her hand and spoke. "Whut deed yoo see?"

"It's private. It was just for Maggie. I gave her what I wrote and let myself forget. Sometimes I remember bits and pieces of a starsong, but usually, after I write it all down, it leaves my head and I can't remember, especially if the message is meant for someone else.

"Anyway, my singing releases an energy into the world... or draws it to me. I'm not exactly sure how it works. I've been told there's a science to it, but to me, it's just what I do. Because I sang, the Unnamed Ones were able to figure out where I was. There were about a dozen of them, and though I tried to fight them off, one of them shot me with a tranquilizing dart.

"The next part your dad tells better, at least all the stuff he did to find me. He had friends who believed in aliens and scary government plans and who could do all sorts of stuff on computers and with machines—it's all as magic to me as my singing is to them. But he found me.

"So, the Unnamed Ones wanted me to starsing for them, and I refused." Lines around her mouth and eyes grew deeper. "They were not very nice. And when they realized your dad was on their trail, they told me they had caught him and would hurt him if I didn't starsing." Tears glimmered in Zalana's eyes. "Except they hadn't caught him. They were lying to me. I had only just started calling on the stars, stars that I used to think were alien, but that I was getting to know better, when your dad and two of his friends broke in, brandishing guns."

Her mother took a deep breath and let it out slowly, blinking away more tears and finally focusing on Kyra. "You know how I get when I sing, though. Once they interrupted, I all but passed out due to breaking the trance. Your dad carried me out, but one of his friends...he didn't make it. His other friend nearly didn't escape, either. The scar your dad has on his arm is from him pushing his best friend out of the way of a bullet. And I couldn't do anything to help." She shook her head.

"When we tried to go home, we found more people were looking for us. We'd been flagged as terrorists all over Earth. Police and constables from almost every country were looking for us, so we had to stay hidden. Finally, Gerard, your grandfather, and your dad's friend, the one he saved, helped us find our way into a secret facility, where there were ships that could travel out of that solar system. We nearly got caught sneaking in, though." Zalana looked away again.

"Thuh scahr on yoor back?" Kyra offered. Her dad was always the one who told this story. It was different coming from her mother. Dad would talk about all the adventure; Mom remembered different parts. Sadder ones.

Her mother nodded, reaching behind her and wincing, as if it still hurt. "I pushed your dad away. Shoved him into the ship. I didn't tell him I'd been hit—I wouldn't even let myself scream or cry. I told myself he had to concentrate. Last time I had been behind the controls of a ship, I'd crashed it. Your dad was always better with machines, and I wanted him safe. If he was worried about me, he would have taken care of me and they might've broken into the ship and stopped us. I was able to keep from passing out until we had left the planet's atmosphere. Then I just fell over. Fortunately, the ship had a medical pod, designed in case someone without a medical degree was left in charge, so your dad just had to put me into it. That's why the scar is so small."

Kyra nodded. In her dad's version of the story, he always grew worried and guilty at this part because he hadn't seen the blood. Mom had been wearing black and staying away from him. It wasn't until she fell and he picked her up that he knew how badly she'd been injured. He was able to program the pod to save her life, but he knew very little about medicine, so it wasn't perfect. A real doctor or a surgeon could have left no scar.

"Yoo 'scaped, thoo."

"We did." Her mom smiled again. "I was able to tell your dad how to get to my star system and the planet Cordelier, where the Starbard home has always been. Many years had passed between my crash-landing on your dad's planet and my return to Cordelier. With your Aunt Lyza not having the ability to starsing, everyone thought the Starbards were gone for good. But we weren't, were we?"

Kyra shook her head and smiled. "Stihl heer."

"We are. And I'm going to go help the Greens on Caterbree, and I can help all sorts of worlds and people who need me, on any of the planets we can travel to. That's what Starbards do. We help people. It's a big responsibility, but people have avoided wars and been prepared for weather disasters, crop failures, and all sorts of things thanks to the starsong."

Kyra beamed up at her mother. It was awesome that her mom could help all sorts of people. And she and her dad had saved each other's lives, too. She wanted to be part of that so badly. She wanted to hear the stars' songs and help people. *Hear the stars' songs.* Her eyes fell to her quilt. There had to be a way to fix her so she could do that. There *had* to be!

Zalana touched Kyra's chin and she looked up. "But happy ending, right? We're all here, and we're all safe." She leaned over and kissed the top of her head. "End of story, my heart. Now it's bedtime."

Nodding, Kyra carefully edged down under her covers, trying not to irritate her sunburn. Her mother carefully tucked her in. Her father came in after and apologized for letting her stay out so long. Kyra signed that it was fine and she'd be okay soon. "Sleep and heal up," he said, and kissed her good night.

As she drifted off to sleep, it occurred to her she hadn't copied down the poems. *Tomorrow*, she thought. *Tomorrow.*

"This Marne sounds like a nice fellow," Gerard said from across the table. He'd asked her parents if he could take her out to breakfast, just the two of them. He'd spent most of the previous night in their room playing with baby Alyce while Kyra, still recovering from her sunburn even after two whole days, tried not to be jealous. So she was happy that her parents had agreed to the breakfast plans.

She signed in big, excited gestures about her conversations with Marne, and Marne teaching her to speak, and how she had promised to bring back pictures and stories for him. Gerard repeated back, in words and signs, those parts he couldn't follow.

"Wait a minute, what was that one you just did? That sign?"

Kyra paused. "Dad and I made that one up because we did not know another. It is for how Marne and I talk."

"Aaaaah." Her grandfather nodded and made a different sign and mouthed, "Telepathy?"

Kyra turned bright red and broke into a stream of giggles.

"What?"

"Dad uses that sign when he thinks Mom is being crazy," she explained.

"Oh, I see," he said with an amused grin.

"Funny, because Mom does not like Marne much. I wish she did. He is my best friend."

"Why doesn't she like Marne?" he asked.

Kyra shrugged. "Marne said something, before I left, that she thought I was depending on him too much. I do not understand. I started saying words because I can 'hear' them in my head from him, but she does not like how they sound."

"Well, what do they sound like?"

Kyra paused and bit her lip.

"You said 'good night' to me the first time we met and that sounded fine," he said kindly. "What else can you say?"

Kyra looked into his eyes, clear blue like her dad's, and took a deep breath. "Huh-loo, mai neem ez Kee-rah Stahrbahrd."

Gerard smiled, not in amusement, but like her father did. "My dad, who was also deaf, could never say anything. He didn't have a voice. You only started a few months ago? When you met Marne? Well, you impressed me."

Kyra beamed.

A flat-topped robot scooted by the table with a plate of pastries. Kyra reached for one but missed, frowning at the annoying mechanical server. She looked at her granddad, who was shaking his head. "That's the third one that's gone by. I'm quite sure they're supposed to stop. See that spot there?"

Kyra nodded and watched the machine, a little taller than Marne, pause at a similar black spot near another table, where two dark-skinned women plucked sugary treats. There were about six of the machines rotating and serving breakfast. Gerard had gotten them drinks from the bar, but hot food was put on each of the machines regularly, and the machines would stop at each occupied table.

Narrowing her eyes, she scanned the floor and then ducked under the table. Gerard scooted his chair back so he could lean over and look at her. "What are you doing?" he signed to her when she looked up to see him watching.

"I am good at fixing things. It does not know we are here," she signed back, then returned her attention to the table. She ran her slender fingers down the central column, pausing and then declaring aloud, "Ah!"

She moved her first knuckle and thumb up and down an area, working further and further down until she got to the floor, where she pressed her fingertips against the black rubber that moved between the tile crevices toward the black dot. She rubbed until she got about halfway to the dot and stopped. Holding her palm a few inches off the floor, she held it over the wire, then, nodding in accomplishment, returned to her chair, smacking her hands together to get off any dust or crumbs.

Smiling widely at Gerard's confused face, she signed, "It will stop this time."

As Kyra predicted, it did. She eagerly helped herself to the steaming flatcakes atop the machine and began eating.

"That's remarkable, you know," Gerard said, when she was looking at him again. "That you fixed it like that."

Kyra shrugged and continued eating. When she realized that her granddad was waiting for more of an explanation, she put down her fork and signed, "Dad had me help him fix the wall-screen and the sound machine Mom uses to help her sleep. I just figure out wires well."

"That's more than just figuring out wires well...but I'll let you eat," he said, smiling because she had already picked up her fork again and eaten half of a flatcake in one massive mouthful.

She shrugged and tried to smile without losing her breakfast. Her granddad laughed and pushed her glass of juice closer. "Wash that down before you choke on it." Nodding, she did as he instructed. "Did you know they have gardens on the top level of the ship? When we're done eating, let's take a walk there."

1 Pluviose 897

Today was wonderful! Granddad had me draw two pictures of him in the garden so he could keep one. He said I could hold onto the poetry book until we get to Caterbree, too! That's good because I have so much to write tonight that I don't think I can copy down any poems because I'm already too tired, but if I don't write it down I'll forget them.

I drew pictures of lots of flowers, too, some as big as my face in all sorts of colors. The gardens also had tiny little birds that Granddad wrote were hummingbirds because their little wings beat so fast they made a humming noise. He told me to hold my lips together and try and breathe through them, making my voice work and that would be humming. I felt him do it too! Mom must have been humming when she was washing me and putting that stuff on my burn, because that was what I felt.

I *still hurt a lot today, but at least I could walk around. Mom said I had to stay out of the sun, so when we went to the garden, she gave me this big ugly hat that I had to wear and Dad said I had to, too. Even Granddad wouldn't let me take it off, though it looked stupid. He didn't say so, but he didn't say he liked it either. He just said I had to do what Mom said. Grown-ups ALWAYS stick together like that. It's not fair.*

I had to wipe some of that gel stuff off my fingers to write or the stupid pen would have fallen out of my hand.

I really wish Granddad would stay with us on Caterbree, but he said that the starships that carried people over long distances aren't very common and hold a specific pattern based on where the planets were at certain times. If he stayed, he wouldn't be able to catch another starship to the planet he wants to go to for a long time. I said he could come back to Cordelier with us and stay, and he said that would be nice, but we had a life of our own. I said he would be much nicer to visit with over the vacation days than Aunt Lyza and Uncle Antnee and Jez and Mira because Granddad doesn't pick on me. He laughed and gave me a careful hug around the arms because he seems to know how to hug really well, and said that he believed I'd show them someday that they were wrong for picking on me. Dad says that, too, and Dad sticks up for me...but it doesn't help when no one else is around.

I guess grown-ups have things to do: cook dinner, clean, and talk with other adults. Aunt Lyza and Uncle Antnee always say that the kids will be fine together, just let them be and chat with us and blah blah blah. At least I think that's what they say, from the way Dad explains it. I had hardly started learning to read lips the last time we saw them. It was very slow learning at first, too, especially learning Common Cordelieran AND the conversational Saxonic language that Dad speaks. On top of that, Aunt Lyza's family speaks Common Cordelieran differently than Mom does. Dad told me so, because he doesn't always understand them so well either.

I wonder if Marne can shock Jez and Mira if they bother me. Maybe he can say that, if they tell, he'll do something worse? They're older than me, though, so I don't know, and I don't want to get Marne in trouble. Maybe he can lock the door so they can't come in. That might work.

I really wish Granddad would stay with us. I don't think I will ever see him again if he's going to Tulaine, a planet in another solar system, and, eventually, back to Earth. He taught me to draw more things, too, and he wanted to see me fix other stuff the way I fixed the table robots. We couldn't find anything broken, though. They seem to take very good care of the ship, or at least the parts we are allowed to visit. Granddad tried taking us down this one hall to explore, but we got caught and given a very long lecture on the importance of security and safety. I thought we were going to get in trouble, but Granddad spoke with the man and we didn't. He winked and signed we'd find another way tomorrow.

That was a good idea until Mom said I had to study! She gave me a screen with math problems that I had to solve, and then added another program I had to read for history! And history is boring, and I have to finish it all before I can play tomorrow! I thought we were on vacation, but she said I was behind on studying, and since Dad would have time off, he could catch me up. Dad will check the math problems tomorrow, and Mom will give me a quiz on the history. It's not fair!

Granddad did try to argue, saying that he gave me a "biology" (how he wrote it) lesson today. He had me show Mom all the pictures of the flowers with the names he wrote next to them. She breathed out of her mouth fast and said that if I did well on my math and history, then MAYBE (I felt her say it loud) I could study more biology, as long as Gerard gave her a "lesson plan." He promised he would, so now I just have to finish the boring stuff tomorrow. I'll try and do it fast. I started the math and it was pretty easy, but the history was long…and BORING. Why do I have to know how Napoleon was founded? If it were the old stuff, when people were living in underground tunnels and ancient starships, it might be okay, but we finished that part last year and now we're at where more people, humans specifically, arrived and started making a government. And I already finished the starship part too, so all that's left is how they made a government. Does it really matter? Oh well, Mom would say it does if I want to play.

Now I'm really tired and I can hardly read what I'm writing. I'll copy my favorite poems tomorrow. I promise this time!

Chapter 6
Foretelling

"I NEVER...COPY...poems..." Kyra signed, hands shaking as she clutched the book to her chest with her elbows.

"Keep it, love," Gerard said, pulling her into a hug. "It's my gift to you. We may not see each other again, so it's something that will remind you of me."

"And...you?"

He pulled out the picture she drew of him in the garden. Adjusting the book so it made a flat surface, he put the paper on it. "Sign it for me?"

Tears dripped and blurred some of the lines. She tried to blot them without smudging too much. Sniffling, she wrote,

I love you! Don't forget me.
Kyra Starbard

"Thank you," he signed and said. "I love you, too. Remember that, Kyra."

She nodded as he took his drawing, but her hands were still shaking, and she couldn't think of any signs. She held out her book for him.

Nodding, Gerard took the book and pen and wrote. Closing the cover, he handed it back and pulled her into a long hug where she cried on his shoulder. After a few minutes, he let her go, kissing both cheeks. "You be a good girl. Take care of yourself." Tears glistened at the bottom of his eyes, too. "Be good for your parents…" He leaned in close again. "And never forget, you are very, very special," he mouthed, close to her face. She nodded and kissed his cheeks back before he let her go.

Her father took her hand and slowly turned her around as they headed though the large, airy halls of the landing area. Still shaking, she hardly paid attention as she and her family climbed into a silvery sphere with rose-pink, plush seats. It moved without rails and in many directions—not like an electrotram that could only move forward or back. She had to keep turning her head to see the landing where her grandfather stood, still waving. Finally, the transportation sphere turned around a wall and she couldn't see him anymore.

Biting her lip, she opened the book to see his message, neatly scribed on the inside cover:

To my dearest granddaughter,
The stars are singing a special song for you.
Love always,
Granddad

She read it several times, until her tears blurred the words. Nicolas wrapped his arms around her and kissed her head. Closing her book, she leaned back against him, still crying.

8 Pluviose 897 (Nap, -CDLR-)
17 Epona 1337 (New Cymru, Angbritt, -CTBRE-)
Telling time and dates on a different planet is WEIRD! I feel like I've gone back in time and into the future at the same time! Mom

says that Caterbree has old traditions that Cordelier got rid of before the Cordelieran government even took effect. Dad says that Cordelier changed all the years and how they were counted, and he has no idea when Caterbree started counting years because it makes no sense according to the calculations from his planet. I bet Granddad would have helped Dad figure it out; they seemed to have fun figuring out puzzles. Mom said what does it matter, anyway, we should just adjust to the calculations and laws of whatever planet we're on. She says Starbards must obey the laws of wherever they are to the best of their ability, though there are some rules we may be exempt from if they go against the Starbard Code. I asked her what the Starbard Code was and she said she'd teach me someday, when I was older.

If Marne were here, he'd say that what she didn't say was when I was ready to be a Starbard…which she doesn't think will happen. Dad, Granddad, and Marne all do, though.

I don't feel like caring about that now. I'd much rather be outside where it's summer and everything here is SOO BIG!! Bigger than on the starship! Flowers as big as both my arms spread out that smell SOOOO GOOD! And I can't do that until I do my schoolwork, which I don't want to do, so I'm writing in my journal while Dad's grocery shopping with Alyce. Mom's busy meeting with the Greens, who are like prime ministers here, only there has to be a man and a woman and they HAVE to be married…but are also elected, somehow. I don't quite understand it. Homework is on government, again, which is boring, but that's how I know. It was comparing government here, at New Cymru (which Dad's mouth doesn't match with the letters when he says it…or something weird like that!) the capital of the region Angbritt (one of twelve main government regions for the planet) to Napoleon, the capital of the Napoleon region, but also the capital for the whole planet of Cordelier, which has a unified planetary government…and the only planet with a small enough population and livable area to have that kind of government. (See, I'm doing my homework in my journal!)

The homework I'd rather be doing (aside from learning about the plants and animals on the planet) is putting something back together and *making it work again. Dad had me do that to a radio on the starship, and I got to show Granddad. It would be even better if I could do fixing work outside in the warm weather though. There's a HUGE bird outside the window, half as big as me, that's all purple and blue with a GIGANTIC big beak as pink as Marne!*

I'd even rather be practicing talking with Dad. He's more patient than Marne, but it's still harder because I can't "hear" him like I hear Marne. He got me a book, though, that has pictures of where the tongue and lips go with different groups of letters. He got some books in the city district of New Cymru that made him happy.

Anyway, tomorrow Mom's going to begin the Starsinging! I haven't seen her sing since before Alyce was born. I wonder if she gets nervous for being out of practice. Can you practice foretelling? That'd be funny... how would you know if it were the real future or a practice future? What would make something a practice future? That sounds like something Granddad would find funny. I'll save it and tell Dad later. Now, I have to get back to schoolwork...after I draw a quick picture of the big bird.

8 Pluviose 897 (Nap, -CDLR-)
17 Epona 1337 (New Cymru, Angbritt, -CTBRE-)
   (Later)
   DAD GOT ME TWO NEW JOURNALS!! *After I fill this one up, I'm going to keep two separate ones. In one, I'll keep pictures and notes and poems and stuff I read somewhere else or copies of my "good" writing that Mom and Dad make me do, and the other book will have just my notes and journal stuff. Almost done with the stupid government schoolwork. Maybe Dad will take me outside. It's sunnier longer here, too, which I like. Granddad should have stayed. I think he would have liked it here.*

   On the other hand, it might be good that Marne didn't come. The pretty purple bird eats things smaller than itself. Dad showed me the thing he had to buy to keep the birds away when he carried Alyce around.

I couldn't touch it because it made my hand all itchy. He said it made a sound that humans couldn't hear, but scared away the birds. What if one of the birds got Marne? He hears better than people, so he might not be able to carry that thing around.

Dad said things always work out for the best. As soon as I finish answering the stupid questions, we can go outside!

"I've never seen a sunset that color before," signed Kyra's dad, staring at the rainbow waves across the horizon.

Kyra looked away from his hands and back at the sky, shaking her head. They lay on soft, turquoise grass that smelled almost as sweet as sugar. The house was behind them, and when Kyra arched her neck back until the top of her head rested on the grass, she could see her mother standing in the darkened window that covered the entire wall. She held Alyce and waved at them, then made Alyce wave her baby hand. Kyra tapped her dad, who also twisted around to see. Both waved back, giggling, then returned to looking at the sky.

Trees, bluer than the grass, with leaves the size of both Kyra's hands together, grew along each side of the Greens' "country house." Dad had explained that the phrase "country house" meant that the people who owned it came here to get away from the crowded city. The almost-black trunks of the trees disappeared over a cliff three person-lengths away from where Kyra and her father lay. The setting orange-gold sun shone in multicolored shimmers just above the cliff line and made the edges of the tree leaves glow almost purple.

Her father tapped her again and signed above them: "I think…the air above the trees here has more water in it, so it reflects the light like a crystal…prism… Remember that lesson?"

Kyra made a well-practiced affirmative noise in her throat, and her father replied by sticking his thumb in the air and then taking her hand in his. When the sun completely sank and the first three stars of the night appeared, he sat up. She pouted at him and remained lying down. Her dad gently tugged her arm and turned so she could see his face. "You need to get to bed early if you want to spend the day with Mom while she gets ready for the foretelling," he told her.

After two more moments of pouting, Kyra stood, brushing the damp, sweet-smelling sugar grass from her back with her free hand. Twisting so her dad's arm was around her, she leaned on him as they returned to the house.

More stars started to show in the darkest part of the sky. Kyra smiled at them, feeling more of a bounce in her step and energy through her whole body just from seeing them.

The next morning, Zalana found an already wide-awake, showered, and dressed Kyra sitting on her bed, kicking her legs impatiently. "Well, that was easier than I planned. Ready for breakfast?"

Kyra nodded, although by their second day in New Cymru, she had gotten sick of the food. She had never minded eating fruits and vegetables; Mom or Dad served them with every meal…but those were almost *all* anyone ate here! Breakfast usually consisted of a soupy white liquid resembling homemade glue, mixed with some sort of fruit. On a good day, as far as Kyra was concerned, it would be a sweet fruit. Other times—today included—the fruit was a sour, pink citrus that made her lips pucker and her stomach clench. The only good part, as far as she was concerned, was the drink—a sweet, yellow milk that coated her tongue and throat for a few minutes after each swallow.

Nicolas held Alyce and followed them out the front door. Kyra paused, bit her lip, and signed, "I thought it was going to be just Mom and me."

Her father lowered his eyes and shook his head. Adjusting the baby so she sat in the crook of one arm, he awkwardly signed, "She needs to concentrate…and I can translate what they are saying for you. Some of it will be in a language you don't know."

She couldn't keep from letting her face fall, but took a deep breath and shrugged as though she didn't care. After all, who was she to get in the way of the entire planet of Caterbree knowing what their future was? If Mom were distracted, she might not get it right.

Zalana smiled down at Kyra and reached for her hand as they entered a gold transportation orb. Seeing her mother's smile, she forgot her reservations and grinned back. She snuggled under one arm as they sat down, resting against her mother's floral-scented dress, made of a blue material that shone like metal but felt as soft as skin. Nicolas winked at Kyra from across the orb, and she blew him a kiss.

The orb moved faster than an electrotram, so the world flew by in a long blur. The foretelling would take place in the city's capitol building. What Kyra could see as they entered the city took her breath away.

The buildings appeared to be made out of massive crystals. *How did everything on this planet just get so GIGANTIC?* she wondered. What wasn't crystal looked like wood and metal, but never in beams any wider than her dad's arm. Light reflected off everything, making the entire city glisten like a dream.

When the orb stopped and the family disembarked, a group of people dressed in silvery metal awaited them. Kyra looked at her parents for an explanation. "They call that an honor guard," her Dad signed and said. "It's to protect special guests and important people."

Kyra nodded, then stopped. "Protect?" she signed back.

Her dad glanced toward her mom, and their eyes met for a moment, then he shrugged, but it looked forced to Kyra. "Now it's really just for respect. To show they think your mom is very important."

"Oh," she mouthed without sound, watching her Dad switch arms for Alyce and shake out the other one. She knew her dad was not saying something. She couldn't help but consider all the guards and security warnings on the cruise ship to Caterbree. And the newscast scrolls and the faces her mother would always make when someone mentioned the UFC. Even though she'd seen no warning signs about terrorists nor any guards since leaving the IGT cruise-ship station, there seemed to be quite a few guards and soldiers now. And not just around her mom.

The "honor guard" led them from the orb landing strip and into a building with pink and green crystal glass. Kyra expected everything to take on the colors of the crystals, but it didn't. She frowned in confusion, but before she could ask, two people dressed in clothes like her mother's, but in a deep shade of green, approached them. Behind the couple followed more people in more shiny clothing.

As far as Kyra had always been concerned, her mother was the most beautiful person in all existence. Her hair was the same warm shade as her family's expensive wooden dining room table and reflected sunlight as though it had diamonds in it. Her eyes, the same as Kyra's, looked like emeralds. She had rosy, honey-colored skin and walked as though she floated above the ground. Everything about her mother just seemed *perfect*.

The people of New Cymru looked different...their skin was shinier, their eyes bigger, slanted, their hair—and even their eyelashes!—shone like gemstones or precious metals, and they too glided just above the ground, or so it seemed. They were smaller than her parents, a little shorter, and much slimmer.

Their grace made even Zalana seem awkward and... *fat* was all that Kyra could think. Such thoughts made her feel physically ill. The people didn't seem real to her. Like the whole city of New Cymru, the meeting had a dreamlike quality that seemed fuzzy around the edges, ready to disappear just when she reached out to touch it.

The afternoon flitted by in no less of a blur than the landscape outside the windows of the transport orb. Kyra remembered edges of pieces that she knew somehow fit together like a puzzle. The couple dressed in green were, as she expected, the Greens—Greenman Gwydion and Greenwoman Branwen. Behind them had been the leaders of different "Houses" of the city and heads of different committees and their families. Kyra's family received a tour of the building, which was called "Summerland" and was the government center of New Cymru. Most of the sparkling people Kyra met, including the Greens, had homes attached to the building. And the building had a massive tree growing in the middle, along with plants and gardens in just about every room and hallway. She remembered that it was magnificent... but not much else.

Before she knew it, Kyra was sitting down at a long table with her family, the Greens, and the other House Heads, getting ready to eat...again. (She vaguely remembered standing around eating more fruit, vegetables, and some breads earlier that day.) As she expected, the meal consisted of varying courses of salads, some bread, soups, vegetables, fruits, and a dessert course of more bread and more fruit. Most of it Kyra found palatable, even tasty. However, she found it hard to concentrate and enjoy any food, since she knew what was about to happen. She just ate quickly, as though that would make the starsinging come sooner.

Finally, after people in dark red clothing came around a second time with pitchers of hot dark chocolate, Zalana stood up. Kyra took in a deep breath and held it until a dull pain in her lungs reminded her that she needed to keep breathing.

Bowing to each of the Greens, with an honor guard on each side of her, Zalana left the dining room. After a few minutes, the Greens stood, followed by each Head of House. Nicolas took Kyra's hand and stood. They all backed to the edges of the room while the red-clad people removed the food and adjusted the tables and chairs to face the end of the room, where the crystal-inlaid wooden floor lifted into a stage, only a foot or so higher than the rest of the room. Nicolas led Kyra to their seats of honor near the Greens, right in the front row.

Sitting on the edge of her seat, Kyra leaned heavily on her arms over the table. Even a finger-width closer was worth stretching for. Her mother came to the center of the stage alone. A silver robe draped over her shoulders to the floor, and her mahogany hair fell in waves down her back.

She watched her mother's perfect, rose-colored lips move, her bright green eyes light with magic and power. Warmth, energy, happiness, sadness…so many sensations washed over Kyra. Half of her wanted to close her eyes and just feel them, but the other half wouldn't let her tear her gaze away. She hardly noticed the handful of people, clad in a darker blue, who went onstage behind her mother and plucked stringed instruments or blew into wind instruments.

Zalana moved her arms and swayed to tunes Kyra could only touch and see. She remembered this part of the starsong—anyone in the area, during the trance of the Starbard, could see and feel and even hear (for those that could hear) the stars' music, even if they couldn't decipher it like the Starbard. Silver-white, silver-blue, and silver-violet flames and smoke tendrils emanated from her mother, reaching out like shimmering beams toward the crowd. Kyra could feel the people behind her move, sense their silent entrancement falling upon her hands, neck, and shoulders, the same way she could feel someone yelling or shouting. Or, perhaps they *were* yelling, shouting, or singing loudly. She couldn't tell because she didn't look, but logic told her that no one else would dare make a noise while the Starbard sang.

The lights in the room dimmed to a subtle glow and then went out. Her father poked her arm several times before she looked at him. When she did, he gestured upwards. Above her, the glass ceiling opened up and the velvet night sky reached its star arms toward Zalana. The dance between the starlight and Zalana's song created the only illumination in the room.

It felt like time stopped. It was as though the song had barely begun when the starlight untangled itself from the tune her mother sang. The sky lightened a shade as dawn approached. The vibrations that had warmed Kyra's skin, thrumming through her body, faded. She shivered, feeling as if deep winter had settled into the room. Her father thrust a sleeping Alyce into Kyra's arms. With a gasp, Kyra felt as though she was zooming up a deep tunnel, faster than a transport orb, and she had only been slowed into reality by her baby sister's weight. Had she been in a trance or a dream of her own? She didn't dare to consider that.

The sight of her father gathering her mother into his arms came into razor-sharp clarity as she remembered the last foretelling. Like this one, its ending had been abrupt and frightening, with Zalana swaying, barely conscious. Kyra swallowed hard, swooning herself, as utter exhaustion shook her body but feral energy roared in her brain.

The sky lightened even more.

The foretelling had taken almost the entire night, as it normally did, and her mom had to write it down immediately, lest she forget the message she was given. Since her dad was there, it was his responsibility to care for her until the entire foretelling was recorded. Mom preferred Dad to travel with her because of this, but sometimes she'd have to bring someone else she trusted to help her. Only when everything was written down could her mom rest.

Two older women dressed in plum purple quickly came to Kyra's side. One took Alyce from her arms and the other took Kyra's hand. The women led them to a lush pink room with a bed, a crib, and heavy curtains that were drawn closed. Light glowed softly from the rose-colored walls, but they dimmed as the woman tucked in the two girls.

Exhaustion overtook Kyra even as she fought to stay awake. She wanted to record the entire event for Marne. As sleep won over her body, her slender fingers clutched the spine of her journal, half-pulled from the shoulder bag a nurse had carefully placed beside the bed.

10 Pluviose 897 (Nap, -CDLR-)
19 Epona 1337 (New Cymru, Angbritt, -CTBRE-)
I keep falling asleep and waking up with nightmares. But I don't remember anything except seeing the stars dancing while Mom sang, but I'm scared and I feel like I'm falling and then the stars catch me. And Marne's there. Mom can't sleep until she writes stuff, so even though I'm not a Starbard and I can't hear, maybe I won't sleep well until I write something. I'm soooooo tired. I just want to sleep. And I don't want to write everything right now because I'm tired. I can see sunlight just around the edges of the heavy curtains in my room. Alyce is not quite sleeping either, but she's not fussing, thank goodness. I've seen Mom starsing before, but I don't remember if I had a hard time sleeping then.

I just remember the starsinging itself. It was back home on Cordelier, but up in Parsin, which is far north. Aunt Lyza and her (annoying) family were there, but even they were quiet during the starsinging. And I remember all of that perfectly, so I'm not worried about forgetting tonight if I write about it later.

I just want to sleep…

I started to fall asleep again. I can't erase the stupid pencil smudge on my journal! It was stars again, and it was like I was in a little car or tram or something with them. Marne was there again. I felt really sad and really scared and really happy all at once. And I could feel the stars. Like really feel, even though it's a dream. Like when Daddy picks me up and tickles me with kisses all over. But add that in with everything else I described, and then waking up all of a sudden from a loud bang in my head and scary blackness.

Even if I could hear, I'm too young to foretell anyway. Mom said she had her first starsinging, with help from her dad, who was also a Starbard, when she was seventeen! I'm only ten. It's just dreams. Mom would say I just had a really exciting day and my brain doesn't want to turn off.

Anyway, I wrote, so maybe I can sleep. I'll write more in the morning. Mom will sleep for almost a day after she's done writing, so we'll be here for a while.

The Starbard sings.

Chapter 7
Bard-dreams of Home

"...IT'S NOT COMMON knowledge but—" The man dressed in dark-blue and gold stopped and narrowed his slanted sapphire eyes as he saw Kyra watching his lips.

Nicolas turned around and shook his head at her. Cheeks burning in embarrassment—she didn't know she shouldn't be "listening"—she quickly opened her book to add more detail to another drawing of her mother. When she looked up again, she couldn't make out any words; it looked like they were speaking in a different language. Fine, then, she couldn't accidentally know what they were saying, could she? She mentally *hmphed* before collecting herself and erasing a line she had drawn too darkly.

A shadow on the drawing caught her attention and she looked back up. Her mother was leaning over her, staring at the picture. Kyra closed her journal, cheeks hot once more. She'd shown her mom lots of pictures, and her mother had framed many and hung them around the house, but this picture felt more personal. She didn't want to share it yet.

Zalana's green eyes shone at her daughter. Smiling, she said, "It's beautiful."

Kyra smiled back, biting her lip. Zalana took her hand. "Come, say good-bye to the Greens with me, my heart."

"Kyra Starbard, your visit was an honor to our home, our city, and the planet of Caterbree," Greenwoman Branwen said, clasping her hands around Kyra's.

"Indeed, it was," said Greenman Gwydion, repeating the gesture.

"Eet whas an onnor for me, too," Kyra replied carefully, conscious of the movements in her mouth and feeling her mother stiffen behind her. Her father approached and squeezed Kyra's arm proudly.

The Greens smiled, as if Kyra's speech were as normal as anyone else's, then turned to greet her dad. "Nicolas Starbard…"

Biting her lip and feeling herself blush again, Kyra slipped behind her father. A small smile pulled her lips from her teeth, though.

The Greens each embraced Zalana and kissed baby Alyce on the forehead. Kyra, taking her father's hand, inched toward the transportation orb meant to take them to the Heartwater section of the city to board a starship back to Cordelier.

When Zalana rejoined them, she handed Alyce to Nicolas and took Kyra's hand instead, giving her older daughter another brilliant smile. "It will be good to get back home, won't it?" she asked. Excitement made Zalana speak faster, so it took a moment for Kyra to comprehend and nod. Her own thoughts had been on Marne for the past three days. He'd said that she'd be able to sense him while she was gone, and sometimes, at night when she was falling asleep, she had a sense of contentment that *felt* like Marne. Other times, though, she wasn't sure. She had a lot of her own emotions over this trip, and she'd imagined talking with her friend on more than a few occasions when she was by herself, but she wasn't sure how much was in her head. She didn't sense anything *wrong*, though. At least...not when she thought about Marne.

Still, she carefully reviewed all of her notes and pictures that she wanted to show him. Maybe he'd tell her he'd sensed her, and they could talk more about it when she was home, and she could tell him what she'd been thinking if she was really just imagining things. She didn't mention any of this to her mother. The vacation and the long recovery from the starsinging had relaxed Zalana, made her happier, and Kyra wanted that to last as long as possible.

At the starship station, Kyra couldn't help but scan to see if her granddad had, by chance, returned, or decided to see them again. Of course, she saw no trace of him as she sadly remembered that he'd said he would stay on the same ship two Caterbreian weeks ago—or almost a month in Cordelieran time, according to Kyra's journal.

Mom's foretelling had been near the beginning of the vacation. She explained that, because it was a private foretelling, with only a small audience, she had recovered after only a little more than a Cordelieran week's rest. Had it not been so long since she'd read, it might have been even shorter. Some foretellings were public, though, where people from all over a country, or even a planet, migrated to the starsinging; those would often require nearly two weeks' rest or more. The more people who attended a starsinging, the more energy was needed, and the longer her mother, or any Starbard, would need to rest afterward.

Kyra wanted to tell all this to her granddad, who her father had said knew very little about the Starbard culture. Even as they got onto the ship, the girl still stole looks around, to see if she could spy the familiar salt-and-pepper hair. They stopped to eat lunch in the wall-screen lounge. This ship didn't have tables with scenery, people, and animal designs in the wood, but geometric designs instead. Kyra didn't find it nearly as pretty or interesting.

She ran her finger over the surface of their table, connecting all the pieces of wood the same color as her Mom's hair, feeling her parents and baby sister laugh around her. Her dad had ordered her a Shirley Temple, her new favorite drink, but she sipped it carefully, still looking around as though she expected something to happen... something she wasn't sure was good or bad.

Was Marne in trouble, and was this what it felt like? She didn't think so. It didn't *feel* like Marne. It felt...like something else. It prickled against her skin and inside her head, like pinpricks or tiny drums tracing outwards. And it made her a little sick to her stomach.

The feeling had been creeping up on her at odd times since her mother's foretelling, and she didn't understand it. She remembered not being able to sleep after the foretelling, and writing in her journal. When she read her journal, though, she didn't remember writing those specific words. However, that sick, prickly feeling would come back or get worse, so she stopped rereading that entry. The rest of the time, she ignored the feeling or became distracted by drawing, lessons, playing in the gardens with her family, or other journal entries and notes to Marne. It kept coming back, though, always when her mind had had a chance to wander.

The scream sensation hit Kyra first, and she leaped to her feet. Her dad's face twisted in shock and horror. He jumped around the table to grab Zalana. Her face contorted in pain; her fists clenched, pressing against the table. Holding her mother, Nicolas grabbed Kyra's arm hard, making her wince. He was yelling. It took her a moment to understand that he wanted her to take Alyce back to the room.

People crowded them. Kyra raced around the table to her baby sister, who had begun to howl. She fought Kyra and the straps of the child seat. Twice, Kyra nearly fell from taking a stronger-than-expected baby fist to her neck or shoulders.

Dad carried Mom, who was shouting and flailing in his arms. She couldn't read either of their lips to comprehend what they said. Then her dad, red-faced, blue eyes bright with emotion, stopped and met her eye, ordering her to take Alyce to their room.

She'd never had to hold her sister any time other than when she was calm or playful. Getting the writhing toddler out of the wall-screen lounge and through the crowd of people proved an impossible task for Kyra. An older woman in a white jacket commanded the crowd to part for the family, and they finally did. The woman resembled a Caterbreian more than she did a Cordelieran; her hair, even her eyelashes, shone like precious metal. However, she stood nearly as tall as Kyra's father, with shoulders almost as wide. She tried to take Zalana from Nicolas, but the Starbard would not release her husband. With an aggravated huff, the white-coated woman swooped upon the girls, taking Alyce in one arm and grabbing Kyra's wrist in a vise-like grip. They flew through the crowd so quickly that Kyra felt as though her feet only hit the ground every third step. When they reached the elaborate Starbard suite, both girls were unceremoniously dropped into their bedroom. The door closed behind them.

Kyra had figured out how to feel the energy pulses to get the door open, even when it was locked, by her second day on a starship. She didn't try this time, but stood close to the screaming, red-faced, sweat-soaked Alyce, who pounded with both fists against the unyielding metal. Wrapping her arms around herself, Kyra could feel the reverberations of her sister's cries throughout the room. After several minutes of the tantrum, Alyce fell on her butt, lifted her chin, and simply howled. Despite the discomfort of Alyce's volume, Kyra sat behind her and continued to inch closer. She wrapped her legs around her sister, and then her arms, and slowly began to rock the little girl, until she lowered her head and sobbed into Kyra's elbows.

Alyce cried herself to sleep. Kyra was still awake, sitting on the floor, arms numb from holding her sister, when her father finally opened their bedroom door. Both tear-stained and bedraggled, he and Kyra stared at each other for a long time.

"I'm sorry," he said and signed, but it didn't soften the edges of Kyra's glare. Squatting, he picked up Alyce, carried her to her crib, and tucked her in.

Kyra shook the pins and needles from her arms and legs as she awkwardly stood up. Her father faced her again. "I really am sorry… I didn't know what else to do."

"What is wrong? What happened?" she signed. "Is Mom all right?"

"She's fine now, sleeping," he answered, reaching a hand to Kyra. After a pause, she took it and followed him into the bedroom he shared with her mom. Hair messy and face almost as pale as a Caterbreian's, her mother did sleep, at least, but not comfortably. Kyra saw a tightness around her mother's lips and eyes that only happened when she was angry or anxious. Kyra looked up at her dad, who put a finger to his lips and signed that they should let her sleep.

The bedroom door swished closed behind them, and her dad led her to the kitchenette. He heated some milk and honey, dripping a clear liquid into the concoction. He was silent until the milk was scalded and he'd poured out two mugs, adding more of the clear liquid into his own mug. Handing the other cup to Kyra, he sat across from her.

Kyra sniffed the mug and wrinkled her nose at the hint of a sharp scent. Her dad had already begun drinking his, so she sipped. It burned her tongue, but had a sweet aftertaste and warmed her belly.

"Sometimes," he began, when he saw her looking at him again, "after a foretelling, a Starbard will have...extra visions or bad dreams of other things...that won't relate to the place he or she was foretelling for. That's—that's what happened today." He spoke as well as signed so Kyra would understand him well.

The girl lowered her eyes and pondered a moment. "What did Mom see?" she signed.

Her dad shrugged, eyes growing dark. "She wouldn't tell me. She said..." He frowned and shook his head. "She said it wasn't for me to know, or any of us... She'd...she would take care of it when we got back to Napoleon."

When he didn't look back up at Kyra, she said, "Youuu doh'n't beeh-leeve hurr?" She pursed her lips, finding the sounds harder to make, as her lips and tongue moved slower than usual.

Her father looked up in surprise. "Of course I believe her!" he said after a moment, looking genuinely hurt. "Your mother has never lied to me in all the years I've known her! Your mother doesn't lie, Kyra."

The girl paused again to consider his words, her mind feeling heavier. As she thought, her half-full mug slipped from her hands. It crashed to the floor, making both of them jump from their chairs. Fortunately, Kyra still had her shoes on, as glass chunks crunched beneath her feet. Her dad snatched her up, put her back in the chair, and checked to make sure no glass had gotten through the shoe soles. Satisfied his daughter was unhurt, he hefted her onto his back, with her legs looped through his arms, and headed for her bedroom.

She leaned back, pulling on his shoulders. As tired as she felt, something in her stomach made her afraid to sleep. "No! Pleeashe?"

Stopping, he moved her around so she could see his face. He looked very tired too, but also worried. "What is it, love?"

"Dohn't wanna shleep yet. Pleashe?"

"You should…"

"Tehll…tehll me a storree?"

Her dad took a deep breath and turned back around to the kitchen. "Let me clean this up first," he said, setting her back on the chair. Kyra fought to keep her eyes open as he grabbed a nano-rag mop from a drawer and extended its handle. Its floppy tendrils seemed to glow bright green as it sucked up the spilled milk and pushed the glass into a pile. Then, he swept up the pieces and deposited them into the glass-recycling grinder beside the sink.

He smirked at Kyra, who had wrapped her arms around the back of the chair as she knelt on the seat, watching.

"Still awake?"

She nodded.

"Well, I guess you have earned a story, then." He smiled a little and chuckled, though his eyes still looked sad. "What kind of story do you want?"

"Yoo und Mum."

"Mum, is it now?" he grinned. "Did my dad get you saying that?"

"Eezier to saee." She offered him a smile.

"What about me and 'Mum?'" He picked her up with a grunt and carried her, like the heroes on the wall screen carried rescued people—usually girls. She wrapped her arms around his neck and laid her head on his shoulder.

"Ev'rthng. Meeting, greaht ex-cape…"

"Hmm…" He sat down on the main room's dark green couch and arranged her on his lap so she could see his face. "Didn't you just hear these stories from your mom on the way to Caterbree?"

"Again," she signed, deciding her mouth didn't feel like trying to make words anymore. Her tongue felt like it was too big. Even though her eyes really, really wanted to close, she stared intently at her father's lips.

"I was in college for engineering, what I do for the Napoleon government now, though I didn't know I'd be doing it on another planet someday. My best friend, Tom, was trying to get in with NASA or some other space program to study astrophysics—how stars move and stuff. Anyway, there had been a hurricane the day before, and he and I and a few of our friends were walking on the beach at night after it cleared up. There were shooting stars, and there was a rumor one had fallen on the beach, so that beach was supposed to be off-limits." He grinned. "Which means we, and a bunch of other people, were finding ways to sneak onto it. Most, I guess, got caught, but we figured it was late enough to be safe—it was a few hours before sunrise—and we were also sure we were too good to get caught.

"Anyway, we split up. I followed one set of dunes to the far end of an abandoned building that used to be some military fort or something. It was always all locked up. No one had managed to break the lock since I'd been going out there, and believe me, baby girl, we had tried. But, when I reached this old building, the lock was open. Shattered, even! Of course, I had to check it out.

"Your mom was there, hiding, and she tried to beat me up with a shaft of rebar—that's a long, heavy piece of metal used to reinforce concrete walls or floors. Fortunately, I kept her from leaving a big dent in my head…"

Kyra giggled sleepily.

"I caught the weapon and took it away from her, and she ran for another exit onto the beach. I caught up with her, though, when she tripped in the sand and fell.

"She twisted her ankle really badly, and she was pretty scared. I didn't understand why, then, but you see, she had crash-landed the night before, in the hurricane. She'd been in an escape pod from a ship that was attacked and destroyed at the edge of my planet's galaxy, not even in my planet's solar system. She had escaped and the pod had put her into hibernation, so the last thing she remembered was the attack. On top of it all, she didn't speak the same language as me."

Kyra nodded again, settling into her dad's arms at an angle so she could still watch his mouth. She liked how he could still speak slowly, so she could read his lips, even though his eyes were looking into the story he told.

"The language she spoke, though, the Cordelieran language, is close to another language on my planet. One I had studied, so I understood a little of what she said. I thought she must have been hurt pretty bad, though, because the first thing I understood from her, as she was staring into the sky, was, 'The stars are different. What happened to the stars?'" He smiled at Kyra.

Kyra thought of looking at the stars on Caterbree. They didn't look different there, but Caterbree and Cordelier were in the same solar system. And where he came from, he'd told her before, most people didn't even know about the *galaxy* Kyra's family lived in.

"What did you think when you saw the stars here? When you came here?" she signed.

"It was weird... It still is, sometimes. At night, I want to look out and see certain constellations, but I don't. I had them all memorized back home, and here, your Mom still has to remind me of some of them when we go outside to watch the stars."

"Mm-mn-mm..." Kyra gave her dad a grin. She'd caught him and Mom on the roof porch once, kissing, not looking at the stars.

Nicolas poked her in the belly. "If you're gonna tease, you're going to bed, Little Miss." Kyra pouted and signed for him to continue, please. "Well, we were able to talk a little. She asked me how this planet dealt with outsiders. I thought I misunderstood her, but she realized I didn't misunderstand, and she got even more nervous, because she also knew there were planets that didn't like 'aliens'— as in people from other planets, not just nonhumans. She worried my planet was like that, and...well, she was right... Your mom is lucky she is human and looks like the humans that were on my planet."

Kyra nodded. She remembered one of her lessons about the Caterbreians, and how most of them still called themselves "human," though there were groups who wanted to be identified as their own race, because all the changes to their hair and skin and size had been done through science, and their children now could be born and look more like "Caterbreians" rather than like most other humans.

Her dad continued with his story. "But I had this feeling, like I could trust her...and that I had to protect her. So when my friends found us, I made up a story that she was an exchange student from another college in the area. Except from France, not England like I was. I told them her ankle wasn't hurt badly, but she was worried about causing problems." Kyra looked at him with confusion. "She was worried she'd get in trouble," he explained. "So, my roommate was away for the weekend, and I set her up in my room for the night, and I slept on the couch in our common room. She let me help her with all the scrapes and cuts she'd gotten from the crash landing. She was very lucky to not have been hurt more. I wrapped her knee and ankle, and lent her some of my clothes to sleep in.

"I went to check on her in the morning, before my first class, and she was gone…with my clothes, but I didn't mind that. I was more worried for her. I skipped class to go looking for her. None of my friends had seen her, and they told me to let her go." He paused. "But I just had a feeling…"

Kyra understood that; that's why she didn't want to go to bed tonight.

"So, I went back down to the beach. But there were police on the scene, so I parked down the street and sneaked in through the woods like we had the night before.

"She was right in the middle of three cops, standing tall and looking like a queen, but I saw in her face she was scared. So did one of the cops. This tall skinny guy was getting in her face and telling her to speak English—the language we spoke in that country—and she was glaring him right in the eye. I went over to her and gave her a big hug and went on like she was my girlfriend and we'd been drinking lots of alcohol—because that makes people do strange things—and it got us mostly off the hook. I knew the other two cops, so they let us go. Then, your mom stopped to look over her shoulder when some soldiers took some covered pallets off the beach. She looked so sad right then, I gave her another hug, and she put her head down on my shoulder and let me hold her."

"Mmmmn," Kyra said, nestling more on his lap.

"It was strange, watching as they took the pieces of your Mom's escape pod out from our hiding spot in the sand dunes. They should have seen us and shooed us away, but they hardly seemed to notice us. On my home planet, we've got all sorts of stories about 'aliens' and other planets—crazy ones, and some not so crazy, now that I know—but when I was holding your mom like that, and saw them covering and taking all those pieces, it was like I understood everything for just a minute." He stared at Kyra, like he was looking for something in her face, then he just smiled, and more of it touched his eyes this time.

"From then on, your mom and I were almost inseparable. We moved in together after some rearranging with my roommates. She wanted to learn everything about the planet she was trapped on for the rest of her life, and I fell in love with everything about her. The way she looked at things, how she smiled, how she sometimes acted like she was queen of the world..." He chuckled. "It took her a long time to learn English, and I thought I'd be stuck speaking pidgin French forever, but a lot of times, we didn't even need to talk. We just knew...and I kept her secret about being from another planet."

"And the starsinging?" Kyra signed, even though her hands didn't want to move.

"You need to go to bed, love."

"Just the starsinging? Please? P-l-e-a-s-e?" She spelled out the word for emphasis.

"Only if I tell you while you're in bed."

Kyra nodded. Her father took her hand, as he was probably too tired to carry her this time, and led her to the bedroom. He waited outside until she changed into pajamas, and then sat down on the side of her bed.

She reached up and turned the dial on her lamp so she could clearly see her dad's face. He glanced over to see Alyce shifting in her crib but not waking up, then turned his attention back to Kyra.

"Your mom had been on my planet for almost six months when she asked me if I could keep an even bigger secret. Of course I could, I told her, and she got really quiet, as if she still didn't want to tell me. Then, she said she had to show me, but she needed me to promise that I'd take care of her after."

Nicolas made a face, and Kyra imagined him being hurt. He'd kept the secret of Zalana's being an "alien" on his planet, and he'd taken care of her after she had crash-landed.

"Of course I would; then she went on about making sure I didn't interrupt her, but that I must pay attention and know when she was finished...and then she changed her mind about the whole thing. We...had a few arguments and went through the same conversation a few times, when she finally just asked me to sneak back onto the beach with her, at night. I thought—" Her father stopped short and seemed to think for a minute. She saw pink rise to his cheeks. Before she could ask, because he hadn't really included this part of the story ever, he continued. "That was the first night we really kissed. I mean, my friends figured we were...kissing anyway, even though I still stayed on the couch..." His face grew redder, and Kyra gave him a confused look. He bit his lip a moment.

"But that doesn't matter anyway; so, we were at the beach, and your mom gave me a kiss, and told me she trusted me. She made me sit down in the sand, and she took a few steps back and looked at the sky. And then she started singing. It was the most beautiful sound I'd ever heard in my life. It still is…" He stared at the wall, but Kyra felt he was staring into what he remembered. "Imagine you never saw anything like a starsinging in your life, baby girl, didn't even know such a thing existed." He blinked.

"I was seeing magic. The stars just came down to talk to her, dancing around her like silvery streamers. And I could almost touch them myself. The whole beach, the ocean, every grain of sand, every wave…they were all singing with her, and I could…" He paused and looked away.

Kyra touched his arm and signed, slowly because all of her movements were feeling slow now as she was fighting to stay awake. "You could hear them, too."

Her dad nodded. "Mostly, though, I could feel their music beating right into my heart." He touched his chest. "And then…it was over. She gasped and fell into the sand. I wanted to bring her home, but she insisted on writing everything down…begged me to trust her again…and to take care of her. What else was I going to do? So, I just made her drink water and the tea she had made beforehand and put in a Thermos. We stayed there all night and into the morning, when other people began jogging along the water. She just stayed in my arms, writing. I didn't understand most of what she wrote…but she was smiling when she wrote it. Finally, she dropped her pen and her notebook and just lay against me. Her whole body was shaking, so I packed everything up and carried her back to our car. When I put her in the car, she kissed me again, and said she loved me." Kyra's dad smiled. "And I told her I loved her, too. She said she knew, and I kissed her again." He looked at his daughter. "There, now, you promised you'd go to bed."

Kyra gave him a deep, laborious sigh that she tried to not let turn into a yawn, and scooted more deeply under the covers. He tucked her in and kissed her forehead. "And don't you worry about Mom," he assured her. "She's been through worse. She'll be just like her old self in the morning. Promise."

Kyra nodded but felt sleep taking over before Dad reached to turn off the light. Despite the weight of her eyelids, sleep didn't come quickly enough. Within a few minutes of the door closing, Kyra felt that awful feeling creep under her bed like a sloth monster and settle in for the night.

2 Ventose 897

We'll be home in a few days. I can't wait because I'll see Marne and I'll be in my own bed and it'll be home. I can wait to get home, though, because the closer we get, the more nervous Mom seems to be getting. ~~And the more I feel that bad feeling in my skin and in my stomach, too.~~

After her bad vision, she got back to being "herself," like Daddy said, like on vacation. Laughing, playing, drawing…still giving lots of school lessons. It's all funny, though, but not laughing funny. I don't know…it's like there's something I should be seeing but don't, like those pictures that become a different picture if you stare long enough and cross your eyes or something. I never see the other picture that other people say I'm supposed to see. Or sometimes I just see the hidden picture and not the trick part.

I can't say it because I don't know any words or signs for it, and even if I did, Mom would say that everything was fine, like I see her tell Daddy.

She's lying, though. I know she lies, even if Daddy doesn't think so. I pretended to have a conversation with Marne in my head about it, wondering if a part of him really did reach me like it was supposed to. But I can't tell. I still have that sick feeling in my stomach and in my head that seems to be messing with how I felt before. But I know

Dad hates lying the most of any bad thing. When I do something wrong, like eat dessert before dinner or break something or whatever, I get into much more trouble if I say I didn't do it or make up a story or something. So, me and imaginary Marne figured that because Dad loves Mom so much he won't believe she'd do something he thought worst of all, like lying. I bet, when we get back home, real Marne will say just about the same thing but in a different way because he doesn't like Mom very much, though I wish he did.

I wrote down the starsinging and the foretelling. It took almost 10 pages of my journal! I drew 5 pictures for him too; one of them Mom really liked, though I didn't mean for her to see it. Granddad is the only one I showed a portrait to. Dad never saw any of the pictures I drew of him. I worry that people I draw pictures of will say I got it all wrong, so I just show pictures of other people and animals and plants and stuff.

Not much else to write now. Gonna eat dinner and then I have to finish today's lessons. At least they're good lessons about how to build machines and how the wall-screens work and stuff.

Marne sat on the dining room table, savoring the slightly overripe whitefruit. It was his small conceit to sit upon the burnished and expensive hardwood table that he normally wasn't allowed to eat at. He'd considered eating on the cream living room furniture, but really didn't want to push the chance he'd leave any evidence of his "transgression." At least the dining room table wiped clean and wouldn't stain from fruit juice.

Despite his satisfaction at his little rebellion, a sick feeling sat in his stomach that morning. A feeling he'd been having more strongly and more often. Something was worrying Kyra, something big. And he could feel her getting closer.

She would be arriving soon, the Naratsset concluded with mixed emotions.

He hadn't expected to be so excited for the return of the family who "owned" him, but he missed Kyra. His concern for her current anxiety also surprised him. Even more intriguing was the strength of their bond. Several times during the past few months, he'd picked up feelings and images that Marne knew weren't his—a childlike joy associated with the face of an older human who looked like Nicolas; a deep sadness and loss; and true and utter awe followed by complete exhaustion. And now this discomfort, a fear of something unknown. Once in a while, he'd even thought he'd felt her talking to him. When he tried to answer back, though, it didn't *feel* right in his head. Something seemed to be blocking him. Probably his own deficiency…and that hurt, too.

He'd increased the connection he had with Kyra without considering the consequences. Her tears before her family had left, her unconditional worry for his well-being. No human he knew would have felt what she felt, and no human he'd ever met inspired him to care this much, worry this much—well, for someone besides himself. Giants' toes! No other human would have even purchased him without having Adam, the driver, fit him with a repression collar before they left the ship. (For an added price, of course. But none of Marne's prior families had balked at the cost.)

Marne doubted any other Naratsset would have willingly created the bond he had with Kyra; he hardly believed he'd done it himself. He had just wanted to comfort his friend's distress, keep *her* from worrying about him. He most certainly hadn't expected to worry so much for her.

Nicolas had asked him point-blank, the day before the family left, if he would still be there when they returned.

Chewing a bite of the fruit, he remembered the last part of that conversation with the human.

"Marne...will—will you still be here when we come back?"

The Naratsset stared at the human male who watched him, brow knitted in concern and appearing very uncomfortable. Unable to help himself, Marne reached out his telepathy just a little more but withdrew quickly when a guarded sharpness came into the man's eyes. He'd have to just accept his own sense that there were a lot of levels to the question.

"I...hadn't considered leaving. Honestly." He let his own surprise come through in his voice.

Nicolas sighed. "I... We..." He stopped, took a breath, and started again. "Kyra loves you very much. You mean the world to her... and that means a lot to me. You do, too. How you treat her and care for her. It's just...I do understand if...if you..." The man paused once more, squeezing his eyes closed for a moment. When he opened them, Marne felt Nicolas's guard open, too. On purpose. He could feel the human's discomfort with this topic; he could feel...guilt? Nicolas continued. "You're a person. A person...not—not property... Kyra and I both feel that way. Just...if you were not to be here...I'd want to prepare her..."

Marne's mouth hung open until it became painfully clear that the man had no more words to add. A million things ran through his head that he could say. Where would he go? What family would treat him even a fraction as well? How could he even survive on his own in a human world?

What would happen to Kyra?

Not only had he no reason to leave, but he had a reason to stay. Marne returned Nicolas's gift of trust and lowered his own mental guards somewhat. "I am not leaving," he stated in Nicolas's language, the language the man had taught to both his daughters, and that

Zalana still struggled with. He didn't want to leave. He didn't want to leave Kyra.

As Marne worked the rest of the fruit's flesh and juice from its stone seed inside his toothless mouth, he scanned the news on Kyra's old school tablet. Nicolas had reactivated the flat notebook screen and set it up with limited wireless access for Marne so the Naratsset could have groceries delivered, follow the news, and handle any emergencies. He used it to see if he could figure out what might be weighing on Kyra's mind as she traveled back home.

The tabloids were trying to do their own forecasting about what parts of high society could expect Starbard visits upon the family's return to Cordelier. The news reported that Avignon, the continent's second-largest city, had decided to invite the Starbard for a foretelling.

Specific dates were glaringly absent in all publications. In fact, the pages of travel schedules that one might normally link to in any of the publications had been removed and made unsearchable for the past two weeks.

Why?

Marne's hacking skills were limited to easing household drudgery and escaping, not navigating online news scripts. The headlines covered budgets, political rallies about school programs, the winners of the Lunar Derby, visits from "Important People" from other planets, and a side article about the ethics of using the term "alien" for humans visiting from other planets versus using it for nonhumans from other planets. (Marne found himself reading more of that article and, unfortunately, laughing up a piece of the whitefruit at the ridiculous debates. He gave up on reading because Naratssets weren't even mentioned, and he was three-quarters of the way through the article.) There were scandals about DNA manipulation in both dogs and humans for netball, and inane "human interest pieces" about cute human things, like being nice to one another.

There were plenty of good reasons Marne had rarely bothered to follow human current events, but he had a mission. What was he missing? What were the people in power hiding?

His answers came in the trade section. There were tips on avoiding United Foundation Consortium ships, how to negotiate without violence, and where traders could file claims for their losses from UFC encounters. In the classifieds, some ships even sold counterfeit badges and paraphernalia that might make a ship look like it belonged to a UFC ally, if the crew did business within the UFC's jurisdiction. And while Marne didn't normally read a lot, he could pick up on the unspoken "You're all safe and this isn't really a problem" talk. Which usually meant there *was* a problem.

Having spent most of his space travels in storage, Marne's knowledge of the UFC extended to seeing its uniformed soldiers and listening to strained conversations about it. The UFC did little about the Naratsset slave trade, so he hadn't cared one way or another about what was going on.

He regretted that now. Had he paid more attention then, perhaps he'd know more about what threat they posed, so much so that no one wanted to talk about it.

Turning off the tablet and spitting the fruit seed onto the table with the small mess he'd made, he closed his eyes and reached for Kyra. He could feel she was closer. But, as before, when he reached out to communicate, all he seemed to get was a sense of static, like millions of tiny drumbeats, getting in the way of his communication.

He shouldn't be surprised. He was *pink*, after all.

Regardless, and against the headache that the feeling was causing him, he sent that he wanted Kyra to be careful. Stay with her parents. Stay…safe.

Kyra closed her eyes and leaned into the soft hairbrush her mother pulled through her hair. Even better than the brush, she could feel her mom humming. It was softer than the feel of the brush against her scalp, and if she paid close attention, she could feel even the changes of the music. Better yet, it seemed to keep away the other vibrations in her head that made her feel ill when she couldn't ignore them.

Beginning at the top of her forehead, Zalana parted her daughter's light-brown hair down the middle, and Kyra felt her braid each side, close to Kyra's face, like a crown. A sudden stop and tug awoke the girl from drowsy contentment. She felt her mother speak loudly and sharply, and looked up to see Dad staring in surprise at Mom.

"I'm taking a walk. Alyce is napping, and you and Kyra look comfortable," he replied.

Kyra felt her mother's muscles tense. She turned to look at Zalana's face and saw her tight jaw ask, "Don't go?"

"Love…why? I'm just stopping by the lounge, having a drink, maybe playing some jixare… I'll be back before dinner." Nicolas frowned. "Is there something wrong?"

Zalana's face fell. "No…no. I just thought it'd be nice, the three of us…maybe play some circle cards here?"

"We usually do that after dinner. Besides, you're usually busy with Alyce, and I always hog Kyra." He winked at his older daughter. "So I thought it would be nice to let you two have some time together."

"Well…you're right, heart," she said, though her face still showed defeat.

"Are you sure there's nothing wrong?"

"No, no, I'm sure." She smiled weakly at Nicolas. "You need some time, too. Have fun, and don't drink too much?"

Nicolas chuckled. "I haven't drunk too much since our honeymoon, Z, and I don't intend to start. Besides, I don't think the *Callista* crew could take me doing jigs with every moveable object that crossed my path."

Her mother laughed and Kyra felt her muscles relax some. While she mostly understood the words she read from their lips, there seemed to be more to what they were saying than their words. Her mother's hand still clutched Kyra's arm more tightly than Kyra would have liked, but she didn't protest. After her father left and Zalana didn't stop staring at the door, Kyra asked, "Scay-red uf a-nuhther bad foortell?"

Her mother started when Kyra spoke, and stared at her daughter for a long moment. She shook her head, as if something clung to her hair, and replied, "Maybe a little, but you'll help, right?"

Grinning proudly that her mother trusted her, she nodded vigorously. Mom returned to braiding her hair, but Kyra didn't feel her relax or start humming again.

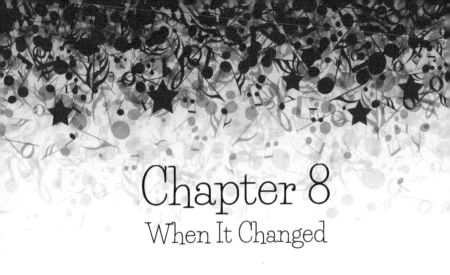

Chapter 8
When It Changed

MARNE AWOKE FROM the corner of Kyra's bed, where he still slept. *Kyra is almost here. And she's thinking about me!*

An unfamiliar beeping in the dining room yanked his attention from that thought and had him all but flying downstairs. Using his telekinesis to boost a hop onto the table, he touched the screen of the tablet and saw a message from Nicolas that confirmed what he'd just realized.

They were disembarking from the InterGalactic Travel cruise ship. They would be back at the house in about two hours, since they were hiring a car and not taking the electrotram.

In a fit of energy, Marne bounced around the small house, cleaning every inch. Because he was not, by nature, terribly messy, and because he'd pretty much kept up on cleaning (with little else to do besides peruse newspapers and watch the wall-screen), the entire house sparkled within an hour of the message.

He sat for the next forty-five minutes on the cream couch, antennae straining to hear a car coming up the long, winding drive to the house. In his mind, he felt Kyra's happiness and excitement dancing around like the streams of bubbles where a family who'd owned him, on the planet Tulaine, had had him wash their clothes…it was one of the few memories he enjoyed from that time, actually. He had been left to himself, and he had found he actually liked the feel of the slippery water in the stream as it would cascade over his hands.

The tablet, still in the dining room, beeped again.

Startled, Marne jumped from the couch and ran to see what the new message said.

"Hi, Marne! Dad showed me how to send this to you! I missed you! See you in 5 minutes! Love, Kyra!"

He pressed his mouth together and felt his antennae twitch even more, as if he wanted to truly hear her already. The sensation of this much…excitement—excitement and *happiness* for seeing a human of all things—was entirely strange to him. He debated reaching out to try and speak with her. She was only five minutes away. He imagined her getting the message, surprised, and then having to explain to her mother that he had spoken to her from that distance. And he imagined Zalana's reaction to him having that kind of link with her daughter.

No, probably not a good idea. Even if he could reach her mind.

Then he heard the whine of an approaching car. Grabbing the tablet and glancing to ensure there was no evidence of his dining-table-sitting transgressions, he rushed to the living room, glanced at the couch to ensure its pristine state, too, and stopped in the center as their laughter approached.

Should he be at the door?

Should he open it for them?

Would Zalana see it as an affront or as a duty he ought to be performing?

He had made no decision by the time their jubilation burst through the door. Kyra slipped by her parents and ran to him.

"Mar-nuh!"

He didn't even flinch when she dropped to her knees—she'd gotten taller!—and wrapped her arms around him. The moisture from her tears slicked against his cheek and he wrapped his small arms around her neck and opened his mind so she could feel what he felt—emotions he couldn't even begin to name.

She pulled back, curiosity slightly muting the goofy grin that bared her white teeth from cheek to cheek.

~I missed you very much, too. More than I think I've ever missed anyone,~ he admitted.

Kyra bit her lip, and he could see her shaking to hold herself back.

~You can hug me just once mo—~

Her arms were around him again before he finished the thought.

~Not so tight, please!~ He couldn't keep from squirming and letting out a squeak. Nic crouched beside his daughter and put a hand on her arm. Zalana, with Alyce in her arms, directed the men bringing in luggage on hover-pallets.

"Everything went well?" Nicolas asked Marne.

"Yes. And the house is clean, and I didn't need all the budget for groceries," he reported.

"Good." He turned to Kyra, and his face helplessly broke into a matching smile upon seeing her glow. "Go unpack and sort your clothes so the dirty ones can get washed tomorrow, and then we'll have dinner, and after that you and Marne can catch up. Okay, love?"

"Yes, Daddy," she said, then managed to beam even more at Marne, who shared his warm approval of her speech.

Nicolas nodded once more at Marne and stood, letting his daughter and the Naratsset run to her room. Despite her father's instructions, Kyra was already projecting the jumble of images from her trip toward Marne, even as she attended to her unpacking and laundry.

Fixing her haphazard sorting, Marne relaxed and enjoyed sharing her adventures in his mind.

Though he hadn't been the one to travel this time, he felt like he was home.

27 Germinal 898

Happy birthday to me! I turned 11 today! Marne is asleep. I put on the little light to write so I wouldn't wake him.

I had a great birthday! I got some new clothes, one of them a pretty dress Mom must have found back on Caterbree because it's that same soft, shiny material that looks like a jewel in the sunlight. I also got new books, more poetry, which I like a lot, and two journals!

Naratssets don't celebrate birthdays, and when Marne found out I was supposed to get gifts, he felt very bad. I asked him when his birthday was and he said he wasn't born, he hatched and there were usually too many eggs to keep track of who hatched when. He was snappy when I asked. He gets that way when he feels uncomfortable or bad. I told him that he didn't need to give me a present; he was already my best friend and, since I don't have any other friends because I don't go to school, that's better than any gift. He didn't like my explanation, so he was snappy all day and avoided me until before bed he said he would tell me a story from his world since I kept asking all the time, and that would be my birthday present. Here's the story as best as I can write it since he "told" it to me like seeing a wall-screen picture:

Why the Giants left Annatat (a place on his planet that's like the whole planet but not really) and their Revenge (a new word I learned that means getting back at someone when they make you angry).

A very long time ago, all over the world (Marne's world), giants, bigger than humans, were everywhere. Because they were bigger, they made all the Naratssets do all the work, like growing food, cleaning, and everything, without paying them at all. They had the Naratssets use their powers to fix things, like fences and machines. At that time, all of the Naratssets were purple or orange and not as powerful as they are now.

The giants were often very mean to the Naratssets, starving them if they didn't work fast enough, hitting them with branches or whips or their hands, which were bigger than full-grown Naratssets. The giants would also eat Naratsset eggs!! Mother Naratssets were only allowed to keep the smallest eggs because the giants wanted to keep the Naratssets smaller and easy to control, or so they thought.

One of the tiniest eggs, though, hatched the first blue Naratsset. The giants thought its color meant that it was weaker than the other ones, so they didn't do much about it as long as it did all the work it was given. That Naratsset's name was Alteru, a name still given to the first hatchling of the first clutch of a pair of Naratssets.

While still a baby, Alteru learned he could move things bigger than him. One time, when a giant was hitting his mother with one of the heavy black tree branches, Alteru made the giant fall over. The giant didn't know what happened except that it might have made the tree angry by breaking a branch, so the giant forgot about Alteru's mother, whose name was Kaihd, and began making amends to the tree. Alteru and Kaihd left and returned to their work.

Later that night, the giant found them and was angry that he didn't finish punishing Kaihd, so he broke into their little hut and began smashing the eggs and her. Alteru got very angry and made a bubble that looked like glass around the eggs, and that shocked the giant when he touched it. Then the giant screamed and grabbed Kaihd, trying to squish her in his hand, but the giant couldn't close his hand all the way. He threw Kaihd across the room, but Alteru caught her and made a wall of the same kind of bubble between them and the giant.

The giant's tantrum brought other giants over. Alteru was getting tired, for he was only a child, so his mother told him to leave the eggs and just keep a wall around them. When he did that, she picked him up in a small bubble of her own and held him in her kaatsin *and ran, as fast as she could, into the woods, deep into the woods where the giants couldn't follow because they would have to break many trees.*

The problem was that no Naratssets ever went into the woods. The trees were friends of the giants. They grew big and tall and bent to the giants' will, giving up their arms and bodies to build houses and fences. Kaihd was very frightened because she thought the trees would catch them and return them to the giants, but, by morning, she learned that the trees did not move on their own. Not only that, but many bore fruit that she and Alteru could eat.

They stayed hidden for many years, not even coming close to any of the other Naratssets because they were afraid of the giants seeing them, especially with Alteru's unique color. In that time, Alteru became better and better with his powers, and he was able to help his mother practice. While she never got as good as he was, she still got better. When he was grown up, he convinced his mother that they should begin sneaking Naratssets out of the giant lands and into the forests where they would be safe. Kaihd agreed and added that they should all learn to strengthen their powers like she had, so they could make the giants leave at least some of the land so the Naratssets could farm their own food. She was still very fond of grains and the grown vegetables even though the tree fruits tasted good.

Alteru agreed and, that night, he snuck into town and found out that there was already a secret group working on their powers in one of the homes. They were led by a female Naratsset of indigo color, almost as dark as Alteru, called Mahad. There were stories about Alteru and his mother that these rebel Naratssets told, only until that moment no one knew if the two had survived running into the woods.

With Alteru returning and assuring them they could live in the woods, and that they could stand up to the giants, Mahad and the other stronger Naratssets helped him devise a plan to sneak out all of the Naratssets, a few at a time, into the woods and train them all.

The plan worked, and because there is little difference in appearance other than color in Naratssets, and because they have a lot of eggs, the giants didn't notice the migration for almost five years, when they found they had to eat fewer eggs if they wanted to keep the same amount of Naratsset workers.

A night came when Alteru and Mahad snuck into town to see the giants carrying weapons and patrolling the streets. They heard screams of other Naratssets. The giants had found the hut where they'd been practicing! The hut was in flames with several young Naratssets trapped inside.

Alteru and Mahad put out the fire with their minds and pulled their friends to safety, healing their wounds—for they had become very powerful by now. The giants saw this and went into a frenzy. Half thought they had angered the trees, which they revered, and the other thought that the trees had been bewitched by the Naratssets. Both groups came to the conclusion that they needed to destroy the Naratssets either as a sacrifice to earn back the trees' approval or to gain back control of the trees.

War broke out as the giants began trying to kill any Naratsset they could find. However, by now, most had been trained enough to stay alive. They all retreated into the woods. The giants stopped when the trees grew too close for them to go in without causing a lot of damage. They roared and threatened from outside the forest's edge.

Kaihd wanted the Naratssets to attack that night, but Mahad and Alteru said there were too many injured, and the giants were so frenzied they fought with three or four times their strength. They spent the night healing the wounded Naratssets that still straggled in from the giants' lands.

When morning came, though, a horrible smell filled the air, along with a huge roar so loud it hurt the Naratsset antennae. Another group of Naratssets came in, black with soot, coughing, and carrying more wounded. They told Alteru and Mahad that the giants had killed twenty of their own and lined the bodies along the tree line and set them on fire, as a sacrifice to the trees.

The Naratssets began to panic but the two leaders calmed them down. In the several years they'd been free, other Naratssets had laid eggs that hatched dark-blue babies, many of whom were almost adults already. (I don't quite understand how quickly Naratssets grow up, but Alteru and Mahad seemed like they were married. Marne didn't mention any wedding or anything though—and Naratssets really do get older a lot faster than humans do—except that Marne said a year on Natarasq was almost three Cordelier years, to his understanding!)

Anyway, Alteru and Mahad and the other dark-blue Naratssets boldly led their people through the woods, putting out all the fires as they walked by.

They reached the line of burning giant bodies. They put out those fires too, then created a wall in front of them, pushing the giants away and making them hurt. The Naratssets walked all over the planet, forcing the giants away from them, for the giants were all foaming at the mouth, ready to kill any Naratset they could reach—but they couldn't reach any!

Finally, the force surrounded the entire planet and the giants were forced to leave all of their lands on the surface and disappear deep inside the planet.

There was one problem, though—the power of the Naratssets upset the balance of the planet, and the giants took advantage of that. From the center of the planet, the giants jumped around and made more fire, constantly pushing the planet of Natarasq toward Starfire, their sun. Alteru and Mahad knew that the planet would be destroyed, so once the first of their children became adults, they took three of them and together created a tower to help focus their power, to keep the giants' movements from crashing the planet into Starfire. From that day on, there must always be five blue Naratssets who focus all their power to keep Natarasq on its orbit. Also, after that, *more and more blue Naratssets were born until almost all Naratsset children were dark-blue, the darker the better.*

I asked Marne if this were a true story, and he said parts were. There really were five Naratssets who kept the planet in its orbit, but they had shifts, switching off. He also said that there were a lot of volcanoes on the planet too, many of which would erupt and change how long some seasons were. And, of course, blue was really the only color a Naratsset should be…at least as far as he knew, but the ship that took him from Natarasq had been pretty full of purples. After he said that, though, he wanted to go to bed. He hates remembering the ship, so I can only guess it was very, very horrible since all the bad things in the story, like the giants eating eggs and burning people alive, didn't bother him much, it seemed.

Wow, this is the longest I think I've written in my journal since writing about Mom's foretelling on Caterbree, which Marne enjoyed hearing about. My hand hurts and I'm tired, so that's it. My birthday is almost over.

Kyra tucked her journal under her pillow. While she was tired, her brain wasn't ready to sleep yet, so she stared at Marne, who was sleeping soundly. The little alien hardly ever slept more than she did, and he almost always woke up easily. She wanted to pet his head or something, like her parents would do when she wasn't feeling well. She felt bad that showing her the story had made him feel unwell.

She thought of Alteru's mom, who seemed to be able to do a lot, keeping Alteru safe. Marne didn't say any of the other Naratssets were pink, but they weren't blue. She also thought of her granddad and her dad, who both thought that someday she'd find a way to be a proper Starbard like her mother. And Marne believed that, too.

While she wasn't sure about ever being a proper Starbard, she wondered if Marne might have found different ways to use his powers that made him stronger than he thought. He'd lived by himself for all the time she was gone. And he'd told her that he had heard her sometimes—and he'd even been able to describe Granddad without her telling him!

On top of all that, he was a great teacher and her best friend. And that had to count for something more than being a snobby blue Naratsset who would sell off anyone who they didn't think was strong enough.

"Kyra, grab your backpack and come on!" her father called. Kyra exchanged a look with Marne. He'd heard a strain in her father's voice, and from the look on Kyra's face, she must have sensed it.

Nicolas and Zalana had been fighting more often, especially whenever Nicolas went out. Only, it seemed the two had gotten savvy to the alien's eavesdropping on them, so they kept their voices down at night. Their fights didn't help Kyra, who had not been sleeping so well herself. Furthermore, in Marne's own telepathic communication with her, he was still sensing that odd static sometimes. And he could tell she felt sick…and something else, but he sensed it wasn't exactly an illness kind of sick. He didn't know what to do about it. Kyra hadn't wanted to talk about it either.

"If you're going to go out, at least take Marne with you." Zalana's voice sounded tired and also strained. Marne looked at her, but she averted her face. More confusion. He could count on his fingers—which were two fewer than humans had—how many times she'd actually called him by his name.

"Sure," Kyra's father replied, staring at his wife for a few moments, but she turned and headed toward the kitchen. Marne sensed Zalana fighting to hide fear and sadness, but not from him. He knew that she knew what he could sense, and she had always been deliberate about hiding it. So why wasn't she hiding it now? "Come on, Marne," Nicolas called from the front door. Marne pulled his attention from Kyra's mother and obediently followed.

By the time they reached the tram, a good long walk from their road and into the suburbs, Nicolas's blue eyes sparkled and he grinned widely, spinning Kyra into a few dance steps before they ascended the stairs to the platform.

"Where are we going?" she signed excitedly, jogging to follow him.

"A surprise," he signed back when they reached the platform, then added aloud, "A late birthday present."

She bounced around him on the platform until he continued. Marne cringed as close to the very center of the platform as possible. There was no chance his limited telekinesis would save anyone if they fell from this height!

"I've been planning it for a while." He smirked as Marne sighed in relief when Kyra stopped moving so she could read Nicolas's lips. "I learned about this back on Caterbree and have been trying to get an appointment since."

"Whut ees eet?" Her voice squeaked. Her excitement rang like a thousand bells in Marne's head. He repressed another sigh, appreciating the joy he sensed from Nicolas, which Kyra magnified.

The tram arrived hardly soon enough for Marne, and Kyra resumed her bouncing as they found seats. She plopped beside her father, leaning on his lap, and Marne hopped on the seat across from them and stretched to see out the window as they left suburban Napoleon and headed deeper into the countryside. Mostly, though, all he could see was the sharp whitish-blue of the Cordelieran sky. He kept his antennae focused on the two humans, though, knowing Kyra would ask him later to translate anything she missed or couldn't remember. And he was rather curious himself.

"Pleeeeeeeeease," the girl begged aloud while signing. Marne noted her advancement in making her voice do what she wanted. He was proud of her. Even though her tone of voice made him wish he could suck his antennae into his head to dull the vibrations.

"Fine, fine, fine," Nicolas finally gave in, bending down to kiss her face several times, making Marne cringe. "There's a group of people who meet in Northern Louvre…some of them can't hear, like you, others can't see, and some just learn things differently. They work together to learn and make things better for people like you, like them, who for some reason or other couldn't or wouldn't conform to school admission standards in most of Cordelier."

Kyra looked at her father, trying to piece together the words and signs for several minutes, but Marne understood perfectly and wondered if Nicolas had intended to expose so much of his politics and opinions regarding this planet, or rather, it seemed, the ruling class of this planet. He wasn't sure if Kyra would understand her father's underlying rebellion, but Marne felt even more respect for the human…and wondered if this was what he and Zalana had been fighting about. As far as Marne could see, Zalana was far more enamored of the Cordelieran government than Nicolas was.

Nicolas told Kyra more about the group, and his zeal made him speak faster and use terms and words that were new to Kyra, so Marne focused on translating for his friend. Keeping their silent communication nonintrusive was quite a bit of work, so he hardly noticed the belligerent conversation in the back of the car. Neither did Nicolas, who still spoke animatedly to his daughter, whose own enthusiasm only fed into his fervor.

The two quarrelers spoke in Ghifish, a Tulainian language that Marne didn't think Nicolas spoke, but Marne knew it well enough from the traders that he didn't have to pull out of Kyra's mind to pick up some familiar phrases. Or their pronunciation of the Cordelieran word for "Starbard."

That made Marne turn more attention upon them. Both were in United Foundation Consortium uniforms. He'd read that some of the group had negotiated for and obtained visas for terrestrial travel on Cordelier, but he had also recognized from the telecasts on the wall-screen that there had been a lot of protests about the visas at the government buildings in Napoleon center, as well as the government buildings in Avignon and even Northern Louvre, where they were headed. The two uniformed humans, a man and a woman, argued over a news article as the other passengers uncomfortably tried to ignore them. Ghifish wasn't one of this planet's common languages.

"Nicolas," Marne said softly, trying to draw the man's attention without alerting other humans.

"One second." Nicolas waved his hand in a dismissive gesture and continued talking to Kyra.

The UFC man flailed a hand-screen around excitedly, and Marne became anxious as the man's emotions grew. The man was talking about wicked magic and the upcoming singing Zalana was scheduled to do in Avignon. The UFC woman turned amber eyes upon Nicolas and Kyra. Especially Kyra.

Marne felt the chill from her gaze upon his friend.

"Nicolas." Marne whispered in case the woman decided to turn her attention upon him.

~Marne?~ Kyra looked at him questioningly. Her father must have said something else she didn't understand, but Marne hadn't been paying attention.

"What is it, Marne?" Nic asked.

Before Marne could respond, the UFC woman stood. Marne jumped across the seats, pushing Kyra into Nicolas. He didn't know why; it was simply what he felt he had to do.

A loud bang and a scream shattered the electrotram's quiet ride. Burning pain sliced through his shoulder.

"Marne!" Kyra shouted, grabbing the Naratsset. Nicolas leaped into the aisle, between his daughter and the two UFC soldiers. He shoved both Kyra and Marne to the floor between the facing seats.

Marne couldn't see, but he heard the sound of more shots and saw Nicolas fall to the ground, red human blood staining his yellow shirt.

"Daddy!" Kyra screamed.

Kyra's dad flailed back to his feet and shoved the bench up and over. With a metal groan, the C-frame it was bolted to bent, flipping the bench and partly shielding Kyra and Marne. It was all Marne could do to hold Kyra back, physically and with his mind. He understood Nicolas meant to protect them. But now Kyra's father was unshielded!

More bullets threw Nicolas to the ground. He looked at the Naratsset. "Help! Her!"

Feeling Nicolas's mind enter his, Marne saw himself and Kyra under the flipped metal bench. Safe from bullets. Mustering all his strength, Marne telekinetically pulled the bench entirely from the frame. The bench thudded against the floor and facing seat. Its curve now hugged them between the floor and the other bench. Nicolas crawled from the open aisle toward them, blood smearing a trail beneath him. Bullets hit the bench but didn't penetrate.

"Daddy! Daddy! Daddy!" cried Kyra in a chant as Marne blocked her way to him. The alien reached out a hand to the man, helping him into their protective cave. Blocking out everything else and hoping he was strong enough that it would actually work rather than render him unconscious from the exertion, he forced a bubble around all three in case the bullets or attackers breached their cave. He didn't know how long it would hold or if it would protect them at all. The tram's squealing brakes only heightened the torturous din and threw them into the hard bottom edge of the still-upright seat, which cut into his burning and bleeding shoulder. The impact broke Marne's control and the energy he'd tried to create. He felt himself freeze and panic. He had failed!

But no more gunshots sang. Only loud voices and shouts and cries. A man and a woman dressed in grey and black uniforms, Cordelieran Transport Security, lifted the bench and began to assure them they were safe while another four CTS guards were carrying the unconscious or dead bodies of the UFC soldiers.

Kyra didn't hear, of course, nor did she even look. She crawled over Marne to her father.

"Daddy, Daddy!" she cried, lifting his head into her lap.

Blood trickled from his left ear and the corner of his mouth. Marne couldn't move when he saw, but Kyra kept chanting. The man's eyelids flickered and Marne felt a surge of relief.

"Kyra," he whispered, his lips hardly forming the words. His hands shook as he reached for her.

Marne watched, feeling everything, recording it because he felt Kyra's mind was unable to do so.

Nicolas looked at Marne. "Keep her safe?"

Swallowing hard, he could only nod. "She's safe."

The human nodded, then looked at his daughter. "Kyra... Remember, there's—there's something out there, bigger..."

"Daddy? Ah-Ah dohn't..." She couldn't make out his mouth movements as more blood dripped from his lips.

"I'll sing to you in the stars, baby girl. I'll sing just for you..."

"Daddy? Daddy!"

Marne stared in horror as his friend reached down to kiss her father's now-unmoving face. He reached out his mind to the man but found only cold, nothing. He'd tried to heal small injuries before on himself and on humans (usually because they ordered him to), but these...these were big. Huge. And the body wasn't responding even to Marne's pathetic attempts. The human was gone. Dead. He reached out to Kyra's mind but couldn't get near the painful whirlwind of fear, so he did the only other thing he could think of.

He reached his small hand to hers. She didn't respond. He inched closer, taking her other hand and pulling her arms around him until she finally embraced him, her tears mingling with the leftover lavender blood on his shoulder, the only thing he'd had the power to heal.

Chapter 9
Black Holes, Empty Space

MARNE PACED BACK and forth in front of Kyra's bed as his friend mechanically brushed her long brown hair, braided it, and made perfect bows of black ribbon to match the black velvet and satin dress. When she paused to look in the mirror, he tried to reach her mind again.

Nothing. Black, empty, almost-nothingness, like the clothes she wore.

Like space.

If he couldn't see her breathe and hadn't watched her eat, even what little food she'd consumed, he would fear she were as dead as her father.

~Kyra, please!~ He tried reaching out to her again.

No response, no acknowledgement. He wrung his three-fingered hands. Without a psychic sense of something, Marne resorted to a physical sensation, even wriggling his six toes and flat feet against the thin rug. Something.

Even in space, he'd felt the humans on the ship, the other Naratssets. He'd felt despair and pain from his race, hate and cruelty from the humans and occasional other aliens, but it was *something* against the emptiness of space. Kyra's mind might just as well have been a black hole.

As they joined similarly black-clad Zalana and Alyce, a stark contrast to the cream furniture in the living room, Marne ducked behind Kyra. At least the terrifying emptiness of her mind provided a buffer against Zalana's mental anguish, which hit his small body like a hundred physical blows. Kyra sat on the couch, next to her mother, leaning her head on the woman's shoulder. Zalana didn't respond. She didn't even hold Alyce, who sat upon her lap in uncharacteristic silence. Marne sat beside Kyra, wishing for once he didn't feel invisible.

The doorbell chime frightened him so much that he actually leapt off the couch, barely landing on his feet when he hit the floor. He looked at the family. Kyra, of course, didn't notice, but neither did Zalana. Alyce looked toward the door and down at Marne. He sensed her confusion at everything, as well as the sadness and pain she reflected from the rest of the family. The bell chimed again and Marne cautiously headed toward the door.

A swish of black velvet, silk skirts, and sharp footfalls, sharp even on the light-blue rug, cut him off. Musky perfume floated in a wake behind Zalana as she answered the door. He looked back at Kyra, whose eyes followed her mother. Marne heard Zalana speaking with at least two other voices outside the door, expressing condolences. Even with them not in close proximity, he sensed ambivalence and something else that made him quickly return to Kyra's side. He couldn't name the feeling; it just aroused his desire to protect his friend.

Zalana led two adults and two other children, who were older than Kyra, into the living room. For a moment, he felt a bolt of discomfort crack the wall of numbness she'd built around herself.

~Kyra?~ He tried again, moving closer to her, assured his instincts were, indeed, justified.

~Aunt Lyza, Uncle Antnee, Jez, and Mira...~ came the reply, though her mental voice ebbed away under waves of returning nothingness. He caught fleeting memory tails of Nicolas yelling at Jez and Mira while Kyra cried behind him.

He didn't need to piece together the memory; Jez, a boy with reddish-brown hair, and Mira, a younger girl with yellow-red hair, caught sight of him and their eyes lit with curiosity and a look the Naratsset knew all too well. He couldn't keep from cringing closer to Kyra as they reached their hands toward him.

So much for protection, he chided himself.

"A Ratsi! Mom, look!" said Jez.

"Why does Kyra get her own Ratsi?" Mira whined.

Kyra snapped back to psychic consciousness and slapped their hands away from Marne. "Leef him aloon!"

About to cry at Kyra's violence, both cousins stopped, mouths agape.

"Well, talking. That's a new one on us!" said the man Kyra had pointed out as Uncle Antnee. He squatted in front of Kyra, an arm around each of his children. "When did this happen?"

Kyra held her head high. "Daddy und Marn-uh tot me!" she declared, speaking slowly and deliberately. Marne sensed her burning desire to speak perfectly.

When Antnee and the other two children laughed, Kyra's hurt hit his stomach hard. He slid off the couch, putting himself between the others and her, ready to *make* them back away if he had to. He didn't have to, though. Alyce came up next to him, her chubby face quite red and green eyes fiery.

"Not s'posed to laugh!" the almost two-year-old chastised. "Daddy says not laugh at Kyra!"

Shock silenced the intruding family once again, and Marne looked at Alyce, slightly taller than he. He wanted to thank her but hadn't a chance. Lyza took her husband's arm and Jez's hand and declared, "We're going to be late for the service. We should go." She glared at Marne as she pushed Antnee and Jez off to wrap an arm around her sister.

Kyra shivered behind Marne but took Alyce's hand and followed them out to the extended hover-car that waited to take them to Napoleon Palace.

Marne did not know what to expect from human death ceremonies. Naratssets burned their dead. The humans and other aliens on the slave starship simply threw their dead into space; he'd seen that enough. Upon seeing all the black regalia, he figured that the typical human death ceremony, at least on Kyra's planet, was much different.

From listening to the conversations (as Kyra faded back into her numb cocoon), he learned that Lyza was Zalana's younger sister and, somehow, not a Starbard. She'd married Antnee, who worked for the city of Avignon and held some sort of honor or usefulness. They mentioned a younger brother, dead along with Zalana's parents, and two aunts and an uncle (to Zalana and Lyza) that were in entirely different galaxies (if they were even still alive) and, therefore, not expected.

Regardless of the lack of family, there was still quite a group assembled at the palace. Through the muddle of people, Marne picked up Nicolas's friends from work, as well as some "Very Important People," like the Intergalactic Ambassador of Cordelier, who watched with her husband from a balcony above everyone else. As the consort of a Starbard, it seemed that Nicolas would have a human death ceremony of high-enough esteem to include almost all of the ruling class. Marne disliked them all, sensing that each one wanted to make sure that Zalana saw them there more than they grieved over Nicolas's death.

Alyce had left Kyra's side and begun tugging on her mother's dress until the woman noticed her and scooped her up. While the people all made room for Kyra near her mother and family, few regarded the girl or even looked in her direction. Kyra hardly noticed; her eyes fixated on the book-sized box that a white-haired woman in black and grey robes presented to her mother, who immediately fell to her knees, sobbing.

Lyza knelt beside her, arms around her shoulders. Zalana encircled Alyce in her arms, pressing her close with her elbows, as she held the box. With Antnee, Jez, and Mira so close, all peering curiously at the box, Kyra had to hover a few steps away.

The robed woman took the box back from Zalana and Lyza pulled her to her feet. Alyce, still standing on the ground, clung to Zalana's right hand. Lyza laced her arm around Zalana's left side, all but holding her up. Kyra glanced covetously toward them, but then returned her attention to the box. She looked a few times toward the woman's lips, but she stood in profile and mumbled. Marne could make out the words but knew Kyra had no chance of understanding, so he began to transmit.

~Tell me later…not now…~ came the whisper of her mindspeech as she once more looked at her mother.

His mouthslit twitched. He felt her wanting to be numb again but failing. She wanted comfort more—something or someone to hold, like her mother's hand. Understanding, Marne reached his hand up to her and she gratefully took it.

~They burned his body and put it in that box,~ she told him. ~Dad's in that box.~

Marne didn't know what to say. All the deaths he'd witnessed before had affected him little. He hadn't particularly cared for anyone who'd died, so he felt no loss at the end of their lives; for some, he'd even felt relief because their deaths ended painful abuse. Nic had been a good person. Marne didn't feel the loss as much as Kyra, but in the moments where she wasn't feeling nothing, he had a deep sense of how much it affected Kyra. More than he could ever think of measuring. The Naratsset was sure that the universe had lost something good.

He listened carefully to everything the presiding human said and memorized all of their surroundings. The woman— Kyra said she was called an "honorée"—stood in front of a wall made of many black bricks with names engraved upon them. Some of the carved names looked like the grooves were filled in with silver, making the names stand out. Directly behind the robed honorée, the name "Nicolas Starbard" was filled in. Above his name was another brick, engraved but not silver-filled, for Zalana. Below were one for Kyra and one for Alyce. Seeing their names sent fearful shivers over Marne's body and he looked back up at his friend. She'd wrapped her other arm around herself and almost hurt Marne with the grip of her hand.

Directing his attention away from the chilling wall, the Naratsset studied the semi-circle of humans around the honorée. Only Zalana and Alyce cried. The rest wore expressions somewhere between mildly saddened and bored. He sensed sympathy from some people, but nothing strong enough to pinpoint the ones who actually cared.

Finally, the honorée finished lauding Nicolas's status as a Starbard consort, a talented engineer, and a gifted musician in his own right. She turned around, opened the silver-lettered drawer, and carefully placed the box inside with a metallic *thunk*.

Marne heard a choked sob from Zalana, who, just realizing Kyra was not near her, looked around wildly. She broke from her sister and, dragging Alyce, fell upon Kyra in a weeping embrace.

Kyra didn't release Marne, so he found himself stiffening in disgust at being caught in Zalana's arms, too. He forced himself to relax as Kyra also pulled him close. Marne heard the drawer close, and Kyra must have felt the sensation because she recoiled as if the wind had been knocked from her lungs. Alyce started to sob also, confused and hyperaware of her sister's and mother's grief. Their emotions weighed heavily on Marne, who guiltily put up a mental wall for fear of being crushed.

When they got home, Kyra went straight to her bedroom as Lyza took Zalana and Alyce to their rooms. She changed into pajamas, crawled up onto her bed and lay on her side, drawing up her knees and hugging her pillow.

~No! Don't do this again!~ Marne demanded as he saw her eyes glaze over.

He had a moment's relief when he felt her defiance as opposed to emptiness, but it didn't last long. She twitched her lips and rolled over, determined not to feel the hurt. Marne blew angrily through his tightened mouth. ~Keeping it inside is not good for you.~

Concentrating, he lifted himself and floated over her, landing cross-legged by her face.

~Don't shut me out!~ he forced into her head.

Her eyes widened, as angry at his mental intrusion as intrigued by his levitation.

After a moment, she replied, forcefully, ~Don't wanna hurt!~

Marne tilted his antennae toward her and moved close to her in a floating hop. She began to put up her mental wall again, so he grabbed her hands, knowing it would startle her back to awareness.

~No one *wants* to hurt,~ he told her. ~But feeling nothing is worse! You scare me when you do that.~

Kyra looked at him for a long time, and he sensed her mixed emotions at his admission. She glanced every so often at his small pink hands, that had to stretch to hold her fingers.

~Please. I don't know how to explain it,~ he admitted. ~But I know it's not good. It feels worse than when you were a whole planet away! And...and...~ He tried to stop his last thought from finishing, from letting her pick it up.

Tears filled her green eyes, shimmering in the starlight that slipped around her curtains. The worsening of her pain let him know he'd failed at keeping that thought to himself before she even projected, ~Like I'm...dead...too?~

~I'm sorry. I didn't want to think that or you to...to get that...~

Kyra sniffled, twisting her head so she could wipe her eyes and nose on her pajamas. Marne made a handkerchief float over from her dresser. For a moment, a look of enchantment broke through the grief. He dropped it on her face, evoking a tearful giggle. She let go of one hand to wipe her eyes and messily blow her nose.

~I'm sorry...~ she told him.

~For what?~ he demanded, though he could see the picture in her head.

~You don't like being touched, and you were right in the middle of me and Mom and Alyce, and I felt you were sick and unhappy but I didn't let go, so I'm sorry.~

Marne shook his head. ~You needed me and I was there. You've done things you don't like when I needed you.~

Kyra gave him a teary smile and quickly drew her handkerchief to her face again. Marne continued to hold her hand with both of his while she sobbed.

He could still hear her crying in her mind when she asked, ~Naratssets remember everything, don't they? You remember...all the stuff you see...or hear...or feel? Anything anyone says to you or anything that happens?~

Marne considered. ~Better than humans, anyway.~

He felt Kyra thinking for a while but didn't intrude. Finally, she mindspoke, ~You saw...you heard what he said...when he was...when he was lying there. He wanted me to know something...but I couldn't... What did he tell me, Marne?~

Her friend nodded slowly. ~I can put it in your head, and you can hear it, like when I tell you stories. Would you like that?~

Kyra shook her head quickly, explaining, ~Not now... not yet... I can't...yet. Just...tell me.~

Marne nodded again; there were many memories in his head he wished he didn't recall so clearly. ~The first thing he said was that you should remember that there's something bigger out there...he wanted you to know... He believed it would protect you.~

He waited, sensing her confusion even before she said, ~I don't know what that means. Do you?~

Twitching his mouth in thought, he replied, ~Only a little. Some humans on some planets...believe in...this thing...this power...sometimes a group of powers...that created them and take care of them... That there's some great plan for their success, like destiny.~

~Do Naratssets believe in that?~

~No...not exactly.~ He felt her waiting for more explanation. ~Our planet has energy; it gives us our power, I suppose, and when a Naratsset dies, the power returns to the planet. The power or the energy...sometimes people talk about it as if it were a person, too. It likes the blues and doesn't like nonblues.~ He shrugged, sending her a sense of loss for a better description.

She accepted that and prodded, ~What else did Daddy say?~

~He said he would sing for you from the stars...a song just for you.~

Kyra didn't reply, but he felt her curl up defensively. He squeezed her hand once again.

~Obviously he knew you'd hear him or he wouldn't have said it.~

She tensed and tried to pull away and roll over once more, but he held her tightly.

~One thing I do know—when I've seen humans die or heard human stories, on any planet or in a starship, everyone believes that whatever they say last is always the truth...is kind of like a little foretelling, without having to sing. Kyra, I know you know that. You read all the human stories and the poems. Kyra?~

The girl sighed in resignation.

Marne scooted closer, so close his thick knees could feel her stomach through the pillow. ~Your dad knew you were something special. He always did. Believe me...I could read his mind.~

Kyra managed a half-smile. ~You weren't supposed to read his mind. He didn't want you to.~

~*Right*. And you never do anything your parents don't want you to do?~

Sniffling again, she smiled a little. ~He always seemed to know... Never let me get hurt. Always there...but not anymore… Marne, now what?~ Her face dissolved into grief and helplessness.

Marne squeezed her hand again. ~I know you think I'm small, but I won't let you get hurt, either. I'll be there for you. I promise.~

She tried to smile again, but she had too many tears still left and her nose still ran, so she wiped her face as she tried to control her breathing.

~Just cry. It's okay. You need to, or you wouldn't have to fight it.~

She nodded but still pressed her face into her pillow. Marne reached one hand and patted her hair as he'd seen Nicolas and Zalana do on many occasions. He sat up with her until she finally fell asleep. Concentrating, he willed her into a deep sleep; this was the first time in four days he'd been able to, and he knew humans needed their rest.

Chapter 10
Asteroid Storm

MARNE FELT SICK when he woke and still sensed the presence of Kyra's extended family in the house. The smell of unfamiliar cooking was sharp, like needles to the olfactory receptors in his antennae. Even Kyra wrinkled her nose in her sleep and rolled over, pulling the blanket over her head. She still slept, and he wanted her to stay asleep for a little longer; he felt physical illness when taking advantage of her emotional and psychic weakness. While he could help fight off the illness some, he was no blue. Blues could keep away infection with just a thought.

Sitting on the edge of her bed, he felt terribly heavy, thinking of the promise he'd made last night, remembering how he'd ducked behind her so many times in fear of Zalana or, just yesterday, the other children. Some guardian he'd make, barely able to lift his own weight, unable to focus in a muddle of thoughts and noises and emotions.

Unable to heal injuries like what had killed her father.

It didn't take long before his vow was tested.

Lyza opened Kyra's door without even a knock. "Kyra! Wake up, breakfast's ready!"

Marne looked at her sharply, mustering up what confidence he could, and said, "She's getting sick from all this stress. She needs sleep. Just save her some food."

"Hmph!" The woman said, glaring at Marne. He sensed she knew enough about "Ratsies" to be wary, but not enough to realize what his color confessed. "Well, the rest of us are hungry and all of us are feeling sick from 'stress.' We all need to eat, so the little princess can find her own breakfast when she's ready."

Marne balled his hands into fists and sent a small charge through the air. Not much, but the woman didn't know that was about all he had.

"Ah! You little…" She trailed off, glaring at him with a mixture of loathing and fear. Then, with another "Hmph!" she turned around and banged the door closed behind her.

Glancing back at Kyra, who was rolling over and making a responsive noise, he locked the door and gingerly patted her head again until she went back to sleep.

"Z, heart, we need to come through the living room to bring the beds in," Lyza said to her older sister. Zalana responded with a half-nod and allowed Lyza to pull her out of the chair and lead her to her room. Lyza looked over her shoulder at where Kyra, Alyce, and Marne were watching the wall-screen. "And you should turn that off and get the baby's bed in Kyra's room," she ordered Marne.

Marne knew she only spoke to him because it was the most efficient way to communicate to the girls. Kyra would "listen" to him, and Alyce had begun following whatever Kyra did. He switched off the television without the remote, knowing that made Lyza uncomfortable, and transmitted the message to Kyra. The girl nodded. "C'mon, Aleese," she said, holding out her hand to her younger sister. Alyce looked up at her aunt, and Marne couldn't repress his amusement at the child's sharp glare.

When they got to Alyce's room, Marne felt his stomach sink. He'd spent almost the whole day using his abilities to try and teach Kyra, despite the noises of the wall-screen and Alyce, as well as keep tabs on the extended family so he'd know if the cousins were coming to cause trouble. Now this? The child's bed was half the size of Kyra's bed but twice the height, with slatted railings on each side. ~*We're* supposed to move this?~

Kyra pursed her lips. ~Maybe can you lift it a little and I'll pull it?~

Marne sent his severe doubts about such a plan to Kyra without words.

~Well, you can at least try!~ she chided.

While his friend couldn't hear his huff, he was quite sure she could sense it. Her pointed glare let him know that.

The crib began to vibrate, then tremble. Kyra stepped away from it and grimaced.

~They ought to be moving this themselves.~ Marne finally said.

~I'm not asking them!~ She frowned.

~You want me to?~

~No! Just…just try again. And concentrate, maybe.~

This time it was Marne's turn to send a sharp glare *her* way. He *had* been concentrating. Nevertheless, he took a deep breath and focused his mind on lifting the crib just half an inch from the floor, just enough for Kyra to pull it across and down the hall to her room.

It vibrated. It trembled. It shook. The side closest to the Naratsset lifted a paper's width from the floor. Kyra winced, but grabbed it, squeezed her eyes closed, and pulled. It slowly inched with her. Alyce, who had been standing in the doorway, clapped her hands and began giggling and jumping up and down.

The crib stopped moving.

"Alyce!" Marne rebuked, rubbing his head and feeling drained from the power use and the distraction.

The younger child stopped and looked between the alien and Kyra. Kyra looked at Marne. ~She didn't mean anything! You don't need to yell at her. Lyza does it enough.~

Marne's mouthslit trembled and he looked down. "Sorry, Alyce," he mumbled.

"S'okay," the little girl said, who sat down and pointed at the legs. "Movies!"

"Huh?" Marne asked and looked at Kyra. ~Movies?~ Kyra shrugged. Alyce toddled over, wrapped her fingers around the circular legs, and began to shake the crib. As she shook it, the alien heard a distinct *click* and a soft humming. A blue light began to glow under the foot of the crib, showing a space above the rug now. Kyra regarded the leg with a mixture of surprise and discomfort. Marne scooted over to Alyce, who was crawling to the next leg and doing the same shaking motion, with much less effort.

Marne audibly groaned and looked up at Kyra, who now knelt beside him.

~Static hover switches. I feel really dumb.~ He looked at Alyce, who was now crawling to the third leg, with a mixture of amazement and irritation. He moved to the fourth leg. The two buttons underneath dimly glowed the same blue as had appeared beneath the two hovering legs. He watched as Alyce sat where she could see the buttons and wrapped her hands so her fingers hit both, then shook it until the blue light appeared underneath. He flicked his two buttons a few times until he turned on the static hover of the last leg. Alyce giggled again and clapped her hands. "Mernuh!" she cried, and got to her feet. Leaning on the crib, she started awkwardly pushing the crib to the window.

"No," Kyra said gently, coming to the other side of the crib. Alyce paused and looked around the corner at her sister. "We ahre gowing to mai room. Okay?" She slowly pulled the crib toward the door.

It took a second for Alyce to understand, but Marne saw a light break over her face, and she quickly replied, "Okay!" and followed her sister. She didn't have much control over her side of the crib, though, and they quickly got hung up on a doorjamb.

"Here, let me help," Marne said to Alyce, who moved over and made room for him with a big smile. "Let's pull it back a little," he said, trying to mold the words to Kyra and the concept to Alyce. Alyce backed up and Kyra pushed. Together, they straightened out the crib and maneuvered it into Kyra's room. Fortunately, Kyra didn't have a lot of things in her room. There were peach-colored shelves built into the wall behind her bed, and a white dresser on the same wall as the door. There was a little trouble when they had to fit the crib between the foot of Kyra's bed and the corner of the closet wall, where Marne's cage had been tucked (and covered with blankets and dirty clothes). After a little back-and-forth, they got it around and beside Kyra's window that looked out over the red-stone drive and between the scrubby gold and green fir trees.

Marne was turning off the static hover on the last leg when Lyza poked her head in the room. She looked at them with an expression similar to the one Marne had given Alyce when she'd started turning on the hover mechanisms. He decided he didn't like being on the receiving end of such a look and resolved to never look at the baby like that again.

"Well, then," Lyza said in a pinched tone. "You still need to get all of her toys out of there before we can move Jez and Mira's beds into that room."

"Of course," Marne said, head lowered, as was proper for a good "Ratsi." "We were just about to do that."

"Good," came the cold response as Lyza left.

He squeezed an irritated noise back into his throat, making Alyce giggle again. Doing his best to mimic a human smile for the child, which only brought about more piercing laughs, he went back to her room and wondered why human children had to make such awful sounds to show their pleasure and amusement.

"Get out of my way, Ratsi!" Lyza snapped, balancing Zalana on one arm. Zalana looked ahead at nothing and swayed in her sister's grip.

He didn't know which terrified him more, the state of Zalana's mind or of Lyza's temper. Nevertheless, Marne stood his ground, but spoke softly. "Please, ma'am, if you are heading to the study, I need Kyra's school books or the next lesson from Nico—from the computer. She's getting behind in her studies."

"She can make do with what she has while she's looking after Alyce," Lyza replied. "Now get out of my way!"

"Kyra can take care of Alyce and still continue her lessons. We've gone over all she has twice, now. Maybe if you just let me get what she—"

"Get out of my way or Kyra's lessons will be the least of your worries!"

Lyza made to kick at him and he jumped out of her way. Behind his mouthslit, he clenched all of his masticular-oration mouth muscles in frustration. He didn't dare zap her while she was holding Zalana—or maybe he should. Perhaps the jolt would also hit Zalana and wake the woman out of whatever mental storm still raged behind her green eyes. The thought came too late. Lyza had already disappeared into the study with her. He debated waiting and confronting the dreaded aunt again, then decided against it. Twice already, Kyra had been punished by being sent to her room without lunch or dinner for his "stepping out of place." Lyza's threat that he would have worse to worry about than lessons wasn't idle. He needed to figure out another way to get Kyra's schoolwork.

The office door opened, and he scurried back upstairs. Kyra lay on her stomach on her bed, slowly and deliberately reading aloud from her grandfather's poetry book. Alyce had also camped out on Kyra's bed. She was arranging her dolls against the footboard and chatting to each one in her high-pitched voice. His antennae shrank toward his head. The child's piercing voice was even more discomforting than the spicy food Lyza *always* cooked, despite the fact that she was *always* complaining about the heat.

Even if he did obtain Kyra's lessons, how could he teach her with Alyce around? He debated telling her that he'd find her deafness a blessing right now, but she'd take it wrong. She'd be either hurt or defensive of Alyce. On the other hand, he was curious as to why Alyce didn't bother Kyra at all. He'd noticed her sensitivity to loud noises, as if they were physical sensations, but she seemed relaxed no matter how much Alyce talked—and the girl talked to everything from dolls to crayons. She even wished each thing a "good night" as she squeezed them into their places on Kyra's shelves, around Marne's cage, and in clear snap-boxes under their beds. The child even apologized to or chided the throw rug when she tripped on it, as if it could hear. Perhaps Alyce didn't bother Kyra because the piercing tone wasn't in anger? It was beyond his reckoning, he decided, and let it be for whatever it was.

Flexing his mouth muscles and sighing, he climbed up onto her bed and sat on a pillow. Kyra looked at him with a hopeful smile. He shook his head. She sighed and shrugged. The Naratsset felt her disappointment before she forced it deeper inside and returned her concentration to her book. She spoke louder, though, so he could hear.

He reached deeply into her mind; perhaps he could share her deafness. Approaching carefully, he felt her curiosity at his strengthened presence, and her permission. Able to focus on only her voice now, Marne listened as she read her favorite poem.

Fah-ther, fah-ther where ahre you go-wing?
O do not walk so fast.
Speak, fah-ther, speak…

Kyra, as well as the rest of the household, even chatty Alyce, was sound asleep when Marne broke into the study. He silently crawled from Kyra's bed and out the door. Having sat in on many a lesson, Marne knew where Nicolas kept the plans and drives for Kyra's lessons. Moving around the furniture, he climbed onto the desk that sat against the wall and beneath a window looking out onto the gardens of many-colored stones behind the house. He found a small memory drive and the next set of lessons for Kyra and copied them. As they copied, he looked at the shelves above the desk, focused on the book-sized tablet on which she did her lessons, and mentally floated it down. He'd just moved the tablet and himself to the floor when the door opened and Zalana stumbled in.

Gasping, he pulled the tablet and himself beneath Nicolas's desk and hid in the shadows. The woman wore a white gown, with a silken green robe hanging loosely over her shoulders. She hugged herself as though caught in a storm, shaking and sobbing.

Zalana stared around the room, probably sensing things amiss but unable to focus. Finally, she staggered toward the chair, falling to her knees and wrapping her arms around the seat. She took in several deep and ragged breaths, as though trying to inhale Nicolas's essence. Marne could still detect the deceased human's scent, but he hadn't thought humans were that attuned to odors.

It seemed Zalana was, though, for she embraced the chair like it was a person, mumbling apologies. Apologies for what, the Naratsset wondered. For the fighting? She spoke incoherently, though, and her mind was no more organized than her speech. That much of a mental disconnect horrified Marne, and he inched farther and farther into the alcove under the desk until his back pressed so hard against the wall it hurt.

Pale morning sunrise brightened the room before Marne felt Zalana in a deep-enough sleep (though still clinging to the chair) that he could sneak back to Kyra's room. He had barely closed her door when he heard the guest room door open and Antnee's heavy footfalls in the hallway. He hid the tablet and memory drives in Kyra's suitcase, kept under the bed with the other storage boxes, before climbing up beside her and making sure she still slept soundly.

14 Messidor 898

I don't think Aunt Lyza's family is ever going to leave.

~~And I'm afraid Mom will never get better.~~ I hope Mom gets better soon.

Alyce plays and draws at her feet when she's "watching" the wall-screen. Aunt Lyza sort of keeps an eye on her then so Marne and I can study. We were looking at Dad's lesson about human bodies, and he was even more interested than me, but it was that icky curiosity like when you see a gross bug but you just can't stop looking at it. He said he didn't mean it that way, but I thought it was funny and I wanted to know what Naratssets look like inside, and he said that if we were meant to see our insides, our skin would be transparent. And then he went on and on about how humans knew all that, and then he went looking through more lessons until he read that, at one time, they used to cut up sick or dead humans, and then he just stopped reading. I thought it was kind of neat, except for the dead part, but I told him when I went to the doctor the last time to check my ears, he made tiny cuts inside to look at something. Marne got all tensed up at that and said there's a reason it hurts when skin is cut; it's not supposed to be cut. I told him that it didn't hurt because they put me to sleep and then I asked him how Naratsset doctors worked. He said that they just thought of things and fixed them...but that the doctors, were, of course, blue, not pink.

Sometimes I worry that Marne feels worse about being pink than I do about being deaf, even when Uncle Antnee and Jez and Mira laugh when I talk. And I know he gets more angry at them than I do when they laugh.

He buzz-shocked Jez once (just a little), when Jez had me cornered and was poking me until I said things so he could laugh. Aunt Lyza, of course, didn't believe me, so she locked Marne in my room and then walked me to bed so I wouldn't try and bring him food. I felt *really bad and suggested we sneak down to the kitchen, but he said that Naratssets don't need as much food as humans do, just like they don't need as much sleep. I asked him what he does when I'm sleeping and he said he just thinks and rests and "No, before you ask, I don't get bored, either."*

I thought Mom was getting better that morning, though, because I wouldn't let Aunt Lyza and Uncle Antnee not let me bring him food in the morning. Uncle Antnee jumped up and screamed at me when I grabbed the eggs and seedfruit off of the counter and then he ran over and blocked my way out the door. He had his hands in fists, and I was almost afraid he might hit me, he was so mad and red-faced, and the veins were big and purple on his forehead. I was brave and stood up to him, but then Mom must have said something because Antnee stopped and stared at her with his mouth hanging open. I looked back and she was looking, really looking, at Antnee, who took a little step away from me, just enough so I could squeeze by. I looked at Mom and smiled, but she just glared at Antnee, so I quickly slipped by with the food before he wasn't stunned anymore.

But Mom wasn't any different for the rest of the day, I think, but she was in her office, so I don't know. It just meant that Marne and I could only do little lessons here and there because we had to keep an eye on Alyce. We started reading her stories, which also were made into lessons for me because Marne would make me read every other page. One time Alyce fell asleep on me, like she used to with Mom, which was kind of a neat feeling except she gets really heavy when she sleeps. I didn't make her move, though. She is awfully cute when she sleeps. Her hair is redder than mine, and it curls. Her skin is also whiter and she has teensy freckles on her tiny little nose.

20 Messidor 898

I have to hide my journal better. I caught Mira in here yesterday lifting up my pillow. She said she was looking for something, and Jez

*said he saw me take it. That made me angry because I NEVER
touch their stuff and they're ALWAYS taking mine and Alyce's
stuff! So I yelled at her, but she just laughed because I probably
said stuff wrong—though Marne says that they shouldn't laugh
because they say my name wrong all the time. Anyway, Marne said
he thought she was looking for my journal. I don't know where to put
it, but Marne said he'd help me make a hiding spot.*

*I asked Jez, one time, when he did his lessons. He laughed, again,
and said he takes the summer off, and Aunt Lyza took them out of
school early when they came here, anyway. Then he called me a freak
because I do lessons at home and can't go to school because they don't
allow defects in school...or stupid alien freaks, either. I was angry
that he made fun of Marne and wanted to hit him, but Marne got
in my head and made me not move. Jez left to go tell his sister what
he said to me.*

*I didn't speak to Marne for a little after that, but then I
apologized. We both knew that Aunt Lyza wouldn't believe that Jez
started it and Mom wouldn't do anything anyway. She didn't before,
either. It was always Dad who stuck up for me when it came to Lyza
and Antnee and Jez and Mira.*

*And now he's gone...and Marne and I can only get into trouble.
I miss Daddy...and I love him.*

*I haven't cried in a while and I don't want to...so I'll stop now.
For now, I'll just put this in my pillow. In the morning, Marne and
I will find a good hiding place.*

Kyra watched in horror as Uncle Antnee used a machine
and hammer to take the lock out of her door. For the first
time since his arrival, Marne had been thrown back in his
cage. She had never felt her friend so furious. He'd made
the saw-machine short almost a dozen times, caused the
hammer to fly out of Antnee's hand a half-dozen more, and

finally resorted to shocking the man until Lyza threatened to throw him, while in the cage, into the ocean.

Kyra screamed and begged and fought until she could hardly breathe as Lyza pinned her hands behind her back. She made Marne promise to stop, and Antnee went back to removing the lock. Alyce screamed from her bed. Kyra could feel those vibrations along with Marne's seething rage. The cage, she learned, muffled his abilities and made him hurt if he used his powers; she could feel that, too. He'd sent the shocks to Uncle Antnee even though it hurt him, and he could hardly concentrate between the cage and Alyce's screaming.

The lock fell to the floor with a heavy *thunk*. "There you go, you ungrateful little brat. See if you take from your cousins again!" Antnee rebuked Kyra, staring her in the face so she could read his lips.

"Ah din't take ehneething!" she declared back, green eyes fiery with defiance.

"Are you calling Mira a liar?" he demanded.

"Yus!" Kyra replied.

"How dare you!" he seethed. "You ungrateful defect! Your Aunt Lyza and I move all the way down from Avignon, take our whole family, so we can help watch you and your sister because your poor mother is sick, and what do we get? What do we get!"

His face, red and sweaty, was only inches from Kyra's. She curled her lip in distaste, feeling his spittle on her. From above, she felt her aunt also yelling. The shouts fell painfully upon her neck and shoulders since she couldn't cover them; Lyza still pinned her arms behind her.

"We get nothing but your lip and attacks by your little Ratsi. On top of that, you have to steal from Mira!"

"Ah din't steal!"

"You filthy little liar!" He raised his hand to slap her face.

"Don't you dare!" Marne yelled from his cage.

Antnee grabbed his hand and fell to one knee, face twisted in pain. After a moment, he got back up. "That's it. I'll drown you like a stray!"

"Noo!" Kyra screamed, twisting and stomping with all her might upon her aunt's foot. The woman yelped, releasing just enough for the girl to yank herself free and get between her uncle and Marne's cage.

~Kyra!~ she heard Marne mindspeak at her. He stopped short, though, and she felt a soft pressure just in front of her. It looked hazy, like heat reflecting off of e-tram rails in Thermidor. When Uncle Antnee touched the haze, she saw the sparks.

"Enough of this," Aunt Lyza said, her watery blue eyes narrowed. "He can't hold that up forever. Ratsies aren't all that strong, and they put them in those cages to sap their power, anyway."

Kyra glared at her, silently warning her that, if Marne failed, she wouldn't be any less vicious.

Lifting her chin, Lyza turned to Antnee, but Kyra could still see her lips. "Go get the kids and take the next tram up to Avignon. School starts in a couple of weeks, and they'll need more things here. Besides, I don't want them in this house for a few days. You don't know what *those two* will do next." She glared at Kyra and Marne.

"We din't do ehneething!" Kyra declared.

"If I hear you spit another lie at us again, Kyra, there won't be anything you or your little pet can do to keep us from sending you off and selling him back to the traders for any price we can get," Lyza said calmly, and turned and left the room. Antnee paused and jutted his chin in threatening agreement before following her out.

As soon as they shut the un-lockable door behind them, Kyra felt the pressure of Marne's force-field drop. Turning to him immediately, she saw him lying on the bottom of his cage, black stone-like eyes looking at nothing.

~Marne! Marne! Marnemarnemarne!~

~I'll be fine...~ came the weak response.

~I'll get you out!~ She ran to her dresser and grabbed some wires left over from when her Dad had given her a light to build. Sitting down in front of the cage, she worked the wires around in the lock for several minutes.

She leaned her left hand on the lock and brightened as she felt something. Adjusting her fingers, she twisted the wire and felt the pop of the lock releasing. Without a thought, she reached in and pulled Marne out. Yanking a blanket from her bed, she wrapped it around him so it was softer than the floor.

While he rested, she went over to Alyce's bed, slid down one of the slatted sides, and lay down beside her little sister, hugging her until she stopped screaming and calmed down. Thumb in mouth, Alyce fell asleep. Kyra smoothed the sweat-curled hair back and covered her with just a sheet before returning to the blanket-nest she'd made for Marne.

She stretched out on the floor beside her friend, staring at him, watching his stomach grow and shrink with each breath. ~Marne?~ she mindspoke quietly.

~I'll be fine...~ came his answer again. ~...won't let them hurt you.~

Kyra sighed and watched him until his pink, wrinkle-less eyelids closed over the black spheres that seemed to suck right back into his skull. After several more minutes, she planted a tiny kiss upon his head, grabbed the rest of her sheets and pillow, and camped out beside him.

It was hard to sleep on the floor, but she wanted to be able to wake up quickly in case anyone came back.

Chapter 11
Defying Orbit

WITH JEZ AND Mira gone for now, Kyra felt a temporary relief and took advantage of it to work "tricks" into her room to warn of any future intrusions. Her door opened inward, so it took next to no thought for her to wedge Alyce's triangle blocks beneath it as a lock while she was inside. Of course, when Alyce, who was just learning to use the toilet, had to go, Kyra would have to scramble or she'd be stuck changing her sister's dirty training diapers.

She also rigged the doorknob with wires that attached to the lights to alert her of someone entering. For times that she was not in her room, she attached the lines to piles of books or more blocks and toys. The trick would be to disengage the traps so she and Marne and Alyce could come and go as they pleased. Alyce, much to Kyra's delight, proved a quick study with the tricks. She had also proved equally unhappy with the occupation of Lyza, Antnee, Jez, and Mira.

Marne had hurt himself more than he would ever have admitted, Kyra realized. He hadn't awakened until late the next morning, and she felt his weariness and pain when they mindspoke. Even though he was awake, he could hardly move. The walls he'd built around his mind felt like physical barriers, but they couldn't contain the disappointment he felt in himself. She said nothing of the feelings and thoughts she detected from him; she knew he didn't want her to know. Even Alyce seemed to give the small alien his space.

Without Marne to translate between her and her little sister, Kyra felt distant from Alyce. The distance, though, helped her learn something quite important—Alyce comprehended far more than Marne normally gave her credit for. It hadn't occurred to her that Marne's prior abusive dealings with humans would have made him underestimate her race so much…including her and Alyce. As she felt his hardly protected emotions and thoughts, Kyra realized quite a bit about her friend. For all she worried about him, thinking about protecting him from the "bigger" humans, he wanted just as much, if not more so, to protect her (and even Alyce, who annoyed him) from the "meaner and bigger" humans.

She thought these things to herself as she brought him Caterbreian rice and broth. Her parents always made them eat rice and broth when they were hurt or sick. They said that bodies could only handle so much at once, and Kyra figured that Naratsset bodies would likely be similar in that respect. They would talk when he was feeling better. It wouldn't be fair, she realized, to bring up things like that now, not when she could feel his emotions like an illness in her own stomach. Had she not told him how it had hurt her feelings when he picked things up she didn't want him to know?

Nearly a full week without Jez and Mira had passed before Marne recovered. Kyra had begun reading entire stories and poems to Alyce. Alyce, it seemed to Kyra, had taken to speaking more slowly and waiting for Kyra to look at her before talking. She was even picking up some of the hand-signs Kyra used.

Kyra was reading from the Blake book when she felt Marne's attention upon her. Kyra looked where he sat on the bed, feet pressed together, black eyes looking at them. She heard, in her head, ~Your speech is getting much better.~

"Thank yoo," she replied. "How ahre yoo feeling?"

~Better.~

Kyra smiled. "Good. I woorried for yoo."

~You shouldn't have to,~ he replied, and Kyra sensed his guilt again.

She shook her head. ~Yes, I should. Same as you worry for me. It's fair that way.~

Marne didn't respond, but she felt his thoughts turn inward as he considered her sentiments. She let him be and resumed reading to Alyce. Alyce, with a quick jerk of her head toward the door, alerted her to Marne's retreat.

"Where ahre yoo going?" she asked.

~I need to walk. I will be back,~ came his answer, as he waved when she tried to stand up. Kyra pressed her lips together, angry at the partial lie she detected. Alyce still held her sister's hand and the book, though, and he had sent a clear signal that he wanted to be alone, so she resigned herself to remaining in her room.

More thoughts and worries swirled around Marne's mind than he wanted, or wanted Kyra to know. He wasn't sure how he felt about how much she now knew, how close their minds had become. They would speak, though. She didn't like secrets, and if he wished to be her friend, he couldn't block her out.

That could all wait, though.

Jez, Mira, and Antnee would soon return from Avignon.

Locking and unlocking doors had become almost second nature to the Naratsset by now, so it took him no effort to let himself into the office Zalana and Nicolas had shared. On the other hand, the appearance of the room, and the emotional imprint, nearly knocked him off his feet. He closed the door behind him and leaned upon it as he stared around.

Hardly any books, all of which Marne knew Nicolas had called "treasures," remained on the bookshelves that had been built into the walls, but that change was pale compared to the almost complete lack of furniture. Marne tried to remember how long ago he had snuck in here to get Kyra's lesson tablet. He shook his oval head several times. The computers that had belonged to both Zalana and Nic had disappeared. Little did that matter; the desks the machines had sat upon also appeared to have vanished. One desk, much smaller but newer, and one portable computer hardly filled the leftover space.

Slowly, Marne walked in a circle around the room, brushing his hand on the walls and built-in bookshelves. He didn't want to touch the new additions; they felt too much like Lyza and Antnee. Piles of papers remained on the floor, and he leafed through them. Bills, transcripts, receipts, letters to and from important people...not in any order, but enough for him to piece together what was going on.

Where were the authorities? Wasn't Kyra's mom a Starbard, honored among the people? Didn't anyone wonder what was becoming of them? Marne considered their situation. They lived on their own land, outside of Napoleon. He didn't know how people contacted Zalana for a starsinging. He'd not been on Cordelier before now, and he had noticed little news on celebrities on this planet. Perhaps there were privacy rules? And if Lyza was closest kin, would they just trust her and whatever she said? Let her do whatever she deemed necessary?

Flexing his mouthslit nervously, he started going through the piles of papers. He had to know what was going on. One was a pile of receipts for items sold, another was late notices for bills, and the third sent a shiver through his spine and *kaatsin*.

In the arguments between Nicolas and Zalana, he'd heard the term "Efficiency Schools." When Nicolas said it, he spat it out like poison. Zalana had seemed to agree with him some. This third pile of paperwork contained several colorful brochures for them. They promised to train students who didn't function well in standard classrooms to fit into society. There were pictures of younger children, some with unusually formed faces or missing limbs, at desks, and older children cleaning inside buildings or in what looked like underground sewers. Menial labor. Stuff he'd be expected to do for families who enslaved him, he noted, just on a bigger level.

Kyra was better than that. She didn't deserve that!

She deserved to hear the stars sing—and that wouldn't happen trapped underground doing slave work for cities.

Feeling almost as sick as when he had seen Antnee ready to hit Kyra, he scrambled out of the room, just barely remembering to lock it behind him so no one would guess his presence. Now what? Lyza's family was bleeding off all of Kyra's family's money—and possibly any future money, if Zalana could ever starsing again. Marne had never seen currency figures as big as the deposit from Caterbree in his *life*! And Marne had worked for some very rich owners. Plus the value of the furniture and books sold? That's why they still remained at the house. Knowing this, Marne felt more emboldened to follow through with his original mission.

He quietly padded down the hallway, cautious of where Lyza might be. The only other place Zalana would be, these days, was in front of the wall-screen. That, of course, was a far more dangerous place for Marne to approach her; Lyza would most certainly hear.

Reaching out his senses, probably more than he knew he should, even now that he was mostly recovered, he searched for Kyra's aunt. In the kitchen. Closer than he wanted, but he didn't have to make any noise to accomplish this. Then again, he didn't know how Zalana would react. Staying acutely alert, he entered the living room.

Zalana stared at nothing in the direction of the wall-screen. Pressing his masticular-oration muscles together, he forced up courage. Any reason to fear this woman paled in comparison to reasons to fear Lyza and her family, for his sake and Kyra's. Marne had no question that Zalana loved Kyra, regardless of whether Marne agreed on how she showed such affection.

He reached into her mind and then retreated, physically flinching.

Time had not soothed Zalana in any way. Her mind was in just as much of a tortured whirlwind as on the day her husband died.

He couldn't do this. He wasn't blue. He had no training. He knew so little about human emotions. Marne had to admit he hardly understood Kyra, and he *cared* for Kyra. Fear and self-doubt rooted him in place.

Hearing sharper than a human's, however, broke through his frozen terror. Feet stepped at the door, three pairs that he recognized immediately. Familiar laughter filtered through as well. The doorbell chimed, and he turned to flee, only to hear Lyza approaching.

Mentally cursing in as many languages as he'd heard on the slave ship, Marne sought a hiding place. With the chair pulled out for Zalana to watch the wall-screen, Marne saw a space behind the cream couch he could squeeze into. In a scramble silenced by more experience than he preferred to remember, he hid.

Lyza greeted her husband and children at the door with hugs and kisses, the same affection Marne had felt between Kyra, Zalana, Nicolas, and Alyce. He couldn't understand it. Antnee picked Lyza up and spun her around while she laughed. He'd seen Nic do the very same to Zalana and Kyra on many occasions. Remaining in the shadows behind the couch, he watched Lyza return her attention to her older sister as she asked Antnee to help her bring Zalana to her bedroom. More gently than he expected, the two adults lifted Zalana, allowing her to lean on their shoulders, and walked her out. Jez and Mira waited until they were out of the way and rushed upstairs.

Worried they would immediately barge in on Kyra, Marne threw caution to the wind and ran to her room. Relief filled him as he heard the two cousins in the room they shared, Alyce's old room. He didn't bother to listen to the conversation as he heard Lyza and Antnee right behind him, walking Zalana up the stairs to her bedroom. Marne quickly ducked into Kyra's room, where she had tucked Alyce into bed.

She met his eyes and he looked away. Eye contact enhanced her communication abilities, something that made little difference between Naratssets. He flinched at the hurt he felt from her at his leaving without warning. Closing his eyes, he slid down against the door and rested his head in his hands.

~I'm sorry,~ he managed.

He heard Kyra sigh and listened to her footsteps approach him. Even though he closed his eyes, he felt her physical presence, but not as much as he felt her mental one. She sat and waited.

~Jez and Mira are back,~ he thought to her.

~I know.~ She tapped her hand on the floor, indicating she'd felt them come up the stairs.

~Your father...would want me to protect you. Keep them from hurting you.~

Kyra shook her head, even though his eyes were closed; she knew he'd feel her sentiment. ~*You* want to protect me.~

He looked up quickly, his eyes meeting hers. ~He asked me to! On the train. That's all he wanted...was for me to help you!~

The impact of his thoughts hit Kyra harder than he'd intended or expected. He lowered his small head again, feeling worse since he knew the memory pained her so much. He heard her sigh again and scoot closer.

~Then, yeah. But he never wanted anyone to hurt, ever. Not me, not Mom, not Alyce, and not even you.~

Marne looked up again. Her lips were set firmly as she stared. He couldn't think of any words to reply with. She didn't know...

~No, I don't know what you've been through. You won't tell me...and that's fine. It hurts you to remember, and I don't want you to hurt, but you think all humans are like that, like the ones who hurt you, and they're not! You think I'm different because I didn't want to see you hurt, and you want to make sure I stay safe and different. And you think if people are horrid to me, then I'll end up horrid just like them. You think Dad only bought you because I asked him to and you don't understand why. You think that he might have been different because he wanted to protect me, too. But he wasn't. Not all humans are bad. It's the different ones who are the bad ones. Most are really good and we care about each other and our families and our friends, and you are afraid to believe that because…because…~

Kyra stopped her thoughts and Marne regarded her for a long time, shaking. She stopped because she felt his pain, he knew, as he watched her pull back and bite her lip.

~You're right.~

~Marne——~

~No. Hurting is normal for both our races. You don't know something's wrong if you don't hurt. Anyway, you're right, mostly, I think. All the stories I know from my people, families defend each other for no other reason than they are family. Except me. Mine didn't. And, yes, it hurts because I know it.~

~It's not your fault!~

Marne folded his arms. ~And it's just as easy for me to believe that as it was for you to believe your parents didn't fight so much because of you.~

~But if I weren't deaf——~

~And if I weren't pink!~

Something lit in Kyra's eyes that made Marne stop talking. Tears came, but he sensed her realization. She lowered her head, and he understood it for a nod. She sniffled and closed her eyes. A single tear dripped from each one.

~It's not fair, and it's not right,~ he continued. ~But I am afraid that you're going to get hurt, like I did, and I don't want that ever!~ He stood up and began to pace. ~And all I've seen is that you end up as one or the other, either the person getting hurt or the one causing the hurt.~

Kyra swallowed. ~Dad never wanted anyone to hurt… and he didn't let people hurt him or anyone else.~

~And you and I are doing such a wonderful job of not getting hurt,~ he thought bitterly.

~I don't understand you when you talk like that! It doesn't make sense when you are saying something that it doesn't feel like you mean.~

Marne sighed. Of course, she wouldn't understand. ~Sometimes...saying it differently makes things hurt less.~ He shook his head. ~But to make it any clearer to you would bring you all the closer to being hurt or doing the hurting.~

"Marn-uh!" She stared at him. "Yoo're not being fair t'me. And *that* hurts!"

Marne lowered his head again, closing his eyes. The only time Kyra didn't say what she meant was when she simply didn't know how to say it, when her thoughts and emotions were too complex for the language she knew. He knew time passed differently for each of their races, but sometimes he felt much older than she.

She replied to his thoughts. ~That's because you think that older people are the ones who do the most hurting and have felt the most hurt, so they deal with it better by not saying it! But you also told me that not dealing with things, like when I didn't want to hurt when Dad died, *doesn't* make things better.~

Other times, he felt like she knew more than he did.

~When I went away to Caterbree,~ she continued, ~you said I'd be as strong as you are with telepathy. And I am, and now you're angry or hurt at that, too.~

~Please! Stop!~ he begged. He felt her withdraw her mind as if she had been physically touching him, and he shuddered. ~I asked you if you trusted me and you said you did...but you didn't think how much I had to trust you! Up until I met you, every human I knew would have broken my *kaatsin*. They would have...~ He tensed all of his muscles and his mind, unable to state the many things he knew had, and would have, happened to him at the hands of other humans. ~I told you not to be numb after your father died because...because I was afraid of what I felt in your head. I don't know how to say it better than that.~

Kyra frowned. ~But you don't have to actually "say." That's how the telepathy works. I know——~

~Kyra!~ Marne interrupted. ~When you trusted me into your head, you trusted me with everything. I know you and the way you think. You would feel someone else's hurt just so they wouldn't...and you don't deserve to feel even a part of mine!~

Kyra shook her head. ~Then you don't trust me, and everything you're saying to me is all wrong!~

~Kyra, no.~

She turned around, breaking eye contact and putting up her own mental wall. The girl didn't bother to put into mental words what she thought, but, as Kyra had pointed out, Marne could read it clearly. He returned to his seat in front of the door, pulling blocks over with his mind to wedge beneath it as he watched her crawl into bed and roll her covers around her in as protective a cocoon as she had made with her mind.

Marne kept his post until he felt everyone in the house deep in slumber. Part of his mind told him he ought to be resting if he intended to do this, but he at least honestly admitted his inability to rest his mind that night. He removed the wedges from under the door and left Kyra's room, returning the wedges to their position afterward, just in case.

Quietly, he headed toward Zalana's bedroom.

Letting himself in—the door wasn't even locked—he went to the edge of the bed and stood beside her.

~Zalana!~ he mentally shouted into the storm of emotions that was her mind. ~Zalana, wake up!~

Nothing. He tried again. And again. And again.

~Zalana, the girls need you!~

The woman shifted, flinching, in her sleep.

"Nic?" she murmured.

Marne paused, considering. ~If it's Nic you need to hear, then yes.~

Her eyes fluttered and she curled her body tighter. "I'm so sorry! I tried to keep you home, keep you safe... I saw, I saw..."

~Just keep the girls safe for me. The girls need you. Alyce and Kyra, they need you, Z!~ Marne felt ill, impersonating Kyra's father, but if it woke the woman up from her mental stupor...

"The girls? Oh, Nic...the girls!"

~Yes! The girls need you. Lyza's using up all our money. She's going to send them away. Protect them for me, Z! For us, for them.~

The woman's brow furrowed. "Nic?"

Marne felt her doubt. He knew he had little time left to get to her. He didn't know Kyra's father that well. He couldn't navigate human emotions like that. ~Please, Zalana, take care of the girls. They need you back.~ He thought frantically; he was losing her. He knew one thing for sure. ~Please, I had to save Kyra! You can't let them hurt her after that!~

Bright-green eyes snapped open. Her fury threw the Naratsset across the room. He hit the wall with a thud he hardly felt. Terror froze him where he was. "You!" she whispered, sitting up in bed, staring at Marne with a vengeance. "How dare you! Oh, how dare you!"

"It's just... It's Kyra, please, Zalana—"

"You dare address me? Say *my* name? Speak as *my* husband?!" Zalana whispered, leaning forward. Her hiss, the emotions he'd awoken, the powers he hadn't realized she had, pinned him to the wall, hardly able to breathe.

Still, he'd woken her. He had to tell her. "See for yourself, your study, your belongings. They're spending the money you put aside for Kyra...for Alyce. They would have hit her! They still might... I've seen... I know—"

"Get. Out," was all she said, as quiet and cutting as the wind. "Now."

It took Marne a moment to connect his mind back to his muscles and body, but slowly, he edged against the wall toward the door. Zalana's green eyes never left him; he felt their pressure even as he entered Kyra's room and closed the door behind him. He dared not wedge it closed; suppose *she* wanted to come in?

Marne shook so badly, he could hardly walk. He'd offended Kyra, so he didn't even feel right seeking sanctuary beside her. He couldn't bring himself to move to the other side of the room, where his cage leaned by the window, where Kyra, unsuccessfully, had tried to heft it outside. Looking around, he crept over to the foot of her bed and curled up by the posts. He fell into a fitful, exhausted sleep.

Chapter 12
Reading Minds

STILL FRIGHTENED, AND very disoriented, Marne awoke the next day, sore from curling up tightly and aching from having slept on the floor. He cursed himself for becoming too accustomed to a soft bed and not being alert enough. Standing and stretching, he looked around. Neither Kyra nor Alyce was in the room.

Marne panicked. Were they hurt? Had Lyza taken them from a psychotically enraged Zalana? Would Lyza have taken them? Could Zalana have hurt them in her fury?

Heart pounding, he reached out his mind, seeking their presences. He nearly fell over when he sensed Kyra's approach. She opened the door, not bothering to undo her tricks…because she had not bothered to hitch them up. Marne stared at her warily as she beamed at him.

"Yoo're awake!" she said, bringing him oatmeal from downstairs. "Yoo din't have to sleep on the floor, Marn-uh. I just…" She paused, trying to find the right words, then simply gave up and handed him his oatmeal. She couldn't contain her delight. "Mum's awake! She mede breakfust! Marn-uh, everything's going to be okay now!"

The Naratsset gratefully took the food; the exertion of so much power yesterday, after the prior week, had made him very hungry. ~That's good,~ he told her, waiting to eat so he could put all of his effort into making his words sincere. Perhaps it was good. Perhaps it had just been the shock last night that had made Zalana act as she did. Marne could only hope.

"We're gonna go shoppin', tooday, becauze Aunt Lyza and Uncle Antnee had to sell some stuff to pay t'e billz while Mum waz sick for so long..." She paused, lowering her eyes. "Mum said she'd rather yoo wait here... Do yoo mayind?"

Marne shook his head. ~No,~ he replied honestly, despite hiding the reasons for said honesty.

Kyra smiled at him, but he sensed she was still picking up more than he wanted her to. Her reaction bothered him more, though. Rather than fight with him, she appeared to ignore her instinct. Not that he wanted to argue more, not that he wanted her to know everything he thought, either, but he didn't know how to take her behavior. It worried him, but she wished him "good-bye" and rushed out the door before he could say anything else.

Staring down at the oatmeal, he ate only because he worried he might need the strength.

21 Thermidor 898

I don't know.

Mom is up and walking around and playing with Alyce. She has been for almost two weeks now. She talks to me and hugs me, but only if I hug her first. She hasn't kissed me yet, though.

I don't know what I did. I know Lyza lied about me and Marne, said we were troublemakers and that we attacked Jez and Mira, but Mom ought to know better. She must know! She didn't yell or anything, and we weren't punished. Jez and Mira leave us alone now, or Mom yells at them, too. She got into a fight with Lyza once. Marne told me part of it. Only part, though.

Marne's not angry at me, but…I don't know that either. I mean, I know he's not angry, but I don't know what he is. I don't know the right words to describe what I feel from him…as in "sad" or "upset" or I don't know the word, or anything. He's sort of avoiding me, but he still protects me when Jez and Mira come too close. He also keeps up on my studies; Mom hasn't picked those up yet.

Maybe she's going to wait until Jez and Mira go back to school.

Anyway, Jez and Mira will be back in school in a week. I can't wait, though I'd rather they just all leave and go back to Avignon, but now that Lyza changed the school, she says that it's too much hassle to change it again so close, so they are going to stay for the school year. Oh well, maybe, with them at school, things will go back to normal. Maybe Mom will be better. Maybe it's just hard with four kids in the house.

~Why can't you just tell me everything this time?~ Kyra demanded, tears in her bright green eyes.

Marne sighed. ~Come here, then, and close your eyes.~

~Why close my eyes?~

~You still flinch when you see my…~ He paused, hesitant, but she did as she was bidden without further questioning. Even so, Marne felt her tense when she felt the fingernail-hard points moving over her brow, eye sockets, and neck. ~Relax.~

"Mmn-hmn," she murmured. He felt a pang when she flinched as his *kaatsin* pierced her flesh, so he willed the connection to move faster, releasing the brain chemicals that made the experience a pleasant one. Unfortunately, the pleasantness receded quickly as the voices Marne heard echoed within her mind. Marne hadn't wanted to share this.

"Zalana, it's really too much for you to teach both on your own," Lyza said.

"Kyra should still be taught…" Zalana's tone did not come across convincingly.

"Face it, Z, she's as likely to be a Starbard as I am," Lyza replied bitterly.

~Why can't she be a Starbard?~ Marne interrupted.

~Shh! Tell you later~

"—still has the birthmark."

"Yeah, and I can hear. Z, you know there are schools—"

"They're not for Kyra! Nic refused—"

"Zalana!"

"Don't, Lyza, just don't!"

Lyza sighed. "And the contract in Avignon?"

"I…I just can't yet." Zalana sounded as though she were ready to cry. Marne watched Kyra's lips tremble in sympathy for her mother.

"Then how are you going to pay—"

"I'll find a way. I can still teach, you know, I had to do something when…when I was where we weren't welcome, and right after…"

"I know, heart, I know. The thing is, though…if you're going to teach this year rather than starsing to cover the bills, how will you also school Kyra and Alyce?"

"I don't know, Lyza," Zalana snapped. "I'll figure it out!"

"I'm just trying to help," Lyza replied.

"I know, I know," Zalana sighed.

"Just look at the brochures. Maybe Nic was wrong?"

"I doubt it."

"Just look, please? You have to focus on Alyce. We haven't heard from any of our cousins, any of the family, for how long? What if…"

Zalana laughed dryly. "What if we're the last? You think I haven't thought of that?" Kyra's mother snorted. "I've also thought maybe things would be better without Starbards." Kyra gasped upon hearing her mother say that. Marne felt her tremble as Zalana continued. "That's why, you know, Ly. That's why they…"

"Hush, sweetie, hush. People like that find any excuse."

"Hmph," Zalana huffed, but followed it with a sniffle. "And since when were you a defender of foretelling?"

"I'm not, but I see no reason to blame yourself for something you have no fault in. For the sins of terrorists!"

They paused. "I don't know, Ly… I mean…" Zalana sighed. "Not my fault. I tried…"

"Shhhhh…"

Soft crying ended the conversation.

~Please stop, Marne,~ Kyra requested.

Marne stopped the transmission and brought back the pleasant feelings as he withdrew his points from her head, healing the small holes they made. The two said nothing for several minutes as Kyra sniffled. He leaned toward her and gently held her feet since her hands were dabbing tears and inspecting the small punctures.

~Do Naratssets bleed when you do that to each other?~

~No,~ he replied, humoring her wish to not talk about what he'd just shared. ~We have receptors in our heads and bodies that open up for it. The only time we make each other bleed is if we're trying to hurt each other.~

~Oh.~ She fiddled with one of the tiny scabs.

~Don't do that; it'll bleed again.~

~Sorry.~

~You want to go to bed now?~

~Yeah.~ Kyra continued to sniffle as she stood up and listlessly rolled into her bed, leaving room for Marne.

~Just 'cuz your parents are Starbards,~ she explained as he settled in beside her, ~or one of them is, doesn't mean you are. You have to have the mark...and green eyes. I think we all have green eyes. Mom's dad was the Starbard and he had green eyes, too, and Alyce has green eyes. I don't think the mark does anything, but it means that some things are turned on in your mind so you can understand the stars when they talk to you. Aunt Lyza doesn't have the mark or green eyes, so she's not a Starbard, and I think Mom got more attention growing up because she was, and Lyza is still angry about that.~

~What's the mark?~

Kyra lifted up the side of her pajama shirt. Just above the waistband of her pants was very dark pigmentation in the shape of a seven-pointed star. ~Seven is a special number, too,~ she added. ~But I don't remember why. They said, I remember once, that it's the darkest ever, so I guess darker is supposed to be stronger.~ She pulled her shirt down with a sigh and another sniffle.

~Maybe you are stronger. Too strong for just using your ears,~ Marne suggested, but she shrugged and rolled over. She felt him edge closer and rub her head.

~Thank you,~ she said. He sensed her smiling, appreciating the fact he still didn't like a lot of touching.

~You're welcome.~

"Kyra!" Zalana chastised. "It's not like milk hasn't gone up another half-kerr this week!"

"Sorry," the girl mumbled, crouching to wipe up the mess she made. As soon as she stood, she looked at her mother's lips.

"I don't know what I'm going to do with you," the woman said. "I really don't."

Kyra sensed Lyza behind her; she saw Zalana glance in that direction, then back to the mess quickly, her cheeks turning pink. "Ah'm sorry, Mum," the girl repeated, afraid of what her aunt was saying behind her back, but more afraid to miss anything her mother said. Marne, of course, was still upstairs, so he couldn't translate. He was probably hungry, too. Everyone's portions had gotten smaller over the past two weeks, but mostly his. Lyza had suggested cutting a full meal out of his diet and Kyra had been rushing to feed him before anyone instituted that idea.

"I need to go and talk with the school today," Zalana announced. "Kyra, be good for your aunt and watch your sister."

Kyra nodded, trying not to let her fear show. She didn't want to be left alone with Lyza's family again. However, Zalana had been more and more touchy about money, Kyra noticed. From the conversation Marne shared with her last night, she worried which school Zalana was going to—the one she might teach at, or the one she might send Kyra to.

"Does the little alien need that much food?" Lyza intoned as Kyra tried to slip out of the room again. "I mean, it's only the size of a small dog."

"He does need et. He's not a dawg," Kyra declared.

"Kyra!"

She felt her mother's sharp voice and foot stamp, so she slowly turned around.

Zalana marched over and inspected the bowl. Frowning, she said, "Kyra, half that."

Tightening her lips, she took half of the cereal out and put it into a bowl on the table. Without a word, she marched back to her room. "Ah'm sorry, Mernuh. They said..." she mumbled upon giving the few bites of food to the alien.

~Don't worry. It's fine,~ he assured her.

"Mum's goin' out tooh talk tooh a school tooday," she told him.

~The one she plans on teaching at?~ He seemed to eat more slowly than usual, only half-filling the spoon each time he dipped it.

"Ah dohn't know," Kyra said, "but Ah made hur angree three taimes this moorning."

~What was she angry over? My food? I really don't need that much...~

"Yoo still need food. Yoo'd go hungry ef yoo thought it'ud make me nawt get yulled at."

~You'd sit and take being yelled at all day if you thought it'd get me more food,~ he remarked. ~So you made her angry because you care whether I starve or not. What else?~

She grimaced and changed to mindspeak. ~You know I hate that thing you do that isn't a lie or truth but something else that doesn't make sense!~

~Sarcasm? Cynicism? General mistrust of anyone except you...and maybe Alyce?~

~I don't know those first two words, but probably that. You need to stop being that all the time!~

~I'll work on it. Now what else was she upset about?~

~I spilt milk.~

~You spilt milk?~

~You're doing it again! That thing! Sarcanicim?~

~Sarcasm? More like incredulity—which means I don't believe it or she's being totally irrational. She got angry at you because you spilt milk?~

~Milk's expensive, and we don't have a lot of money.~

~Because her little sister spent it all buying luxury items for her spoiled husband and child monsters.~

~Because Mom isn't ready to do any foretellings and Dad's... Well, he's obviously not working...~ She looked away and sat against the foot of her bed. She didn't want to think of how much she missed her dad.

~I didn't mean to hurt your feelings.~

~Never mind!~

~Kyra——~

~Why are you allowed to say "never mind," but when I say "never mind" you just have to know what's wrong?~

~Because I *know* what's wrong, and you usually do too, when it's me.~

~Whatever.~

The alien fluttered his mouthslit, which Kyra recognized as a sigh. ~What was the other thing?~

"Hmph!"

~You said there were three things she got angry at.~

"Ah sed, 'Hmph!'"

Marne paused and sighed once more. ~The difference is I know you want to talk about it and I *really don't* want to talk about some things.~

~Maybe I *really don't* want to talk about this! You'll just be sarcasmic again.~

~Sarcastic, not sarcasmic. And I'm not being sarcastic; I'm angry at them, and I don't believe they should treat you like that.~

"Hmph!" she snorted again, then continued, ~Well, I really don't want to talk about it!~

Marne set his bowl down and scooted around so he sat in front of her, his feet pressing against each other and short arms folded. ~Or you're just intent on teaching me a lesson for having private thoughts I don't want to talk about.~

~I already know what you're going to say, anyway,~ Kyra told him. Part of her wanted to look away, but she couldn't keep from watching him out of the corner of her eye

~Maybe I'll surprise you. I think I've managed to do that at least a few times,~ he offered gently.

~I asked her how she was.~

The pink alien blinked. ~What?~

~I asked her how she was and she said she was fine and wanted to know why I was asking and what I thought was wrong…and her voice and—and her eyes were mad at me. But I could just be…be seeing things or worried about things because of what she and Aunt Lyza were talking about last night.~

~Maybe not. I doubt it, anyway. You're quite perceptive.~

"Huh?" She spoke to communicate on top of her sense of confusion at what he said.

~You know things, sense things, feel things. I told you before, when we first met, I hadn't expected you to pick up my thoughts, but you did. You're sensitive…naturally empathetic.~

Kyra shrugged. ~It made her angry.~

~People like to keep their inside thoughts and feelings to themselves. That's what I keep saying about me.~ He did his best to smile. The slit he had for a mouth didn't move as much as a human's, though, but only made tiny dents above and below.

As annoyed and hurt as Kyra felt over the whole morning, she couldn't keep from smiling herself whenever she saw him try to smile. It just looked kind of silly on his face. With a sigh, she changed topics. ~We should probably study now before Jez and Mira chase Alyce back up here.~

The alien nodded and telekinetically pulled out Kyra's lesson tablet. She found herself smiling, almost giggling again. She saw him move stuff with his mind almost every day now, but it still always felt like magic to her. He was purposely trying to make her happy, she knew, and she appreciated it.

Chapter 13
Final Countdown

24 THERMIDOR 898
Mom said she is sending me away to school.
And she said she is selling Marne.

Kyra only managed to write two lines in her journal before throwing it across the room. Tears burned her eyes in a constant flow down her cheeks. Her mind raced.

Marne waited upon her bed, staring at her. She sensed his fear. She wanted to console him, tell him everything would be all right, but it wouldn't be. Not like this.

She felt he was afraid of her. The realization hurt like a knife in her heart, and she looked at him.

The pink alien shook slightly. She hadn't spoken to him when she came in; she'd just taken her journal and begun writing. In her head, she'd thrown up the biggest wall she could picture. If he could hide things, so could she! She wasn't ready to talk about this yet.

She took a few deep breaths and formed her thoughts to him deliberately. ~I would never, ever hurt you and I won't let anyone else hurt you, either!~

~Then what's going on, Kyra?~ he asked.

The girl paced, thinking, but keeping him out of her thoughts. Finally, she declared, ~We're running away.~

~What?~ Marne slid off the bed and walked over to her. ~What are you talking about? Kyra, that's ridiculous. You'll get killed out there. It can't be that bad.~

"It is," she said, speaking to signify how serious she was.

~Tell me! What is it?~

Kyra paced, tears still running down her cheeks and lips pressed so tightly in fury that they probably resembled Marne's mouth more than her own. Of course Marne would disagree about running away; he was just as adamant about keeping her safe as she was about keeping him safe. Nevertheless, she had decided her course of action.

~Mom is sending me to that school…and selling you back to the traders. So we're running away.~

Marne had no immediate response for her but froze where he stood. His round stomach heaved more than usual with his breathing; her explanation frightened him even more than her silence, she sensed.

~We have two days to get ready for this. We should pack food and clothes…and maybe find some money.~ Kyra focused her thoughts, consciously trying to think like an adult and not a child anymore.

~Kyra! Kyra, wait. This is crazy.~ Marne interrupted her. ~You can't just run away. It's not safe! Listen——~

"No!" Kyra stared him down. He didn't get a chance to reply before she felt her mother's footsteps coming upstairs. Quickly, she grabbed her journal, thrust it into her hiding spot behind the mattress, and began changing into her pajamas.

Zalana was smiling kindly as she entered the room but bit her lip when she saw her elder daughter's face. She carried an already-asleep Alyce in her arms and tucked her in first before approaching Kyra. "It's for the best, honey. We need the money, and you need a better education than what I can give you."

Kyra jutted out her chin defiantly, crossing her arms over her chest.

Her mother frowned and returned a displeased look. "That's what's going to happen, Kyra. Period. So make the best of it."

With that, Zalana turned and left, not even looking at Marne as she passed him. After her mother shut the door and Kyra felt her walk back downstairs, she gave Marne a pointed look, knowing he could understand her thought even if she couldn't put it into words.

He didn't answer right away. Still angry, she flipped off the light with an angry slap before climbing onto the bed. She didn't lie down, though. She sat, waiting for Marne to join her.

He did; she felt him climb rather than levitate. He only did that when he couldn't concentrate enough to use his powers.

~If we spend all day tomorrow packing——~ she began.

~Kyra! You can't do this. *We* can't do this.~

~Why not?~ she challenged.

~Because—because… You're only eleven years old. We'll get killed out there!~

Kyra held her head up high. ~We can be careful. We'll find my granddad, and he'll take care of us.~

~Kyra, be reasonable…~

~Why don't you trust me?~ she exclaimed in the telepathic equivalent of screaming.

~I do trust you——~

~No, you don't! You've been avoiding me for weeks, and now you'd rather let Mom send you back to the——the market and let me go to that stupid school...~

~No, no, no, no! Kyra, please, please listen to me. I don't want to go back; I'd rather stay with you, but I'd rather go back if it meant you weren't out there, in the world, getting hurt or killed or worse! Kyra, maybe it's better for you. Maybe they'll teach you stuff that——that I can't.~

~If they could teach me stuff or would help, don't you think Daddy would have sent me there before?~

Marne had no response for that right away. After a moment, he quietly started, ~What about...~

~What?~ She sensed the alien's hesitating guard over his thoughts and frowned.

~That school your Dad was bringing you to...when...~

She hesitated, swallowing hard, then shook her head. ~Mom doesn't know anything about it. He said it was a secret surprise. He never...he never told her anything he was trying to do to help me until after he did it.~

Marne stared at her for a moment, and she realized even he hadn't realized how much she knew, *really* knew, about how her parents felt about her deafness.

Taking a deep breath and forcing the pain in her heart away, Kyra continued. ~Besides, Mom isn't going to spend any more money on me. She doesn't even want me around——~

~No, Kyra, that's not true! It's...~

Something in his tone stopped the girl short. She stared at his face in the dim light; he was trembling. When he didn't explain himself right away, she asked, ~It's what?~

~It's not your fault... It's not that she doesn't want you around... It's—it's my fault.~

~It's not your fault. She——~

~It is. That's why she wants to send me back to market. I hurt her... I...~

Kyra paused, feeling Marne's fear like a hammering pain in her heart and head; her own lungs tightened, as she knew his had. He was afraid she would hate him, and that scared him more than going back to the market. ~Marne...~ she began, but he interrupted.

~Let me finish. After...after I was better from the fight with Antnee and Lyza, I was worried about you, so I decided to talk to your mom. I wanted her...I wanted her to take care of you. I wasn't doing a good job. I thought... I thought...~ He shook his head. ~I couldn't get through. She was still all wild about your dad; that's all she could think of...so all I could think of was...was to talk to her like he would...~

~I don't understand~ Kyra said.

~I spoke to her...in her mind...in his voice. Your dad's voice. I just wanted her to listen, to take care of you. Lyza and Antnee were selling all your things, and they were planning on sending you away, anyway, both of you. I just wanted her to hear, to—to take care of you...~

~You pretended you were Daddy?~

~Yes,~ came his soft and sad whisper in her mind.

Kyra didn't know what to think, so she lay down on her bed, her back to him as she kept her thoughts to herself. She felt Marne moving off the bed and she whispered aloud, "Don't go."

She felt him pause, climb back up, and sit.

After a moment, the girl rolled over to look at him. She still kept her mind closed, though she sensed that hurt his feelings. Finally, she asked him, ~I know Naratssets remember things better than humans…but, can you help *me* remember better? With your…your…~ She couldn't think of the word but visualized the spindly appendages he'd connected to her to improve their telepathic connection.

~My *kaatsin*?~ he asked, sending back a more correct picture of his extenders. ~I don't know. Maybe? I've never tried…~

~Will you try for me?~ she asked, sitting back up.

Marne nodded and lowered his head. From the slit in the back of his neck, he extended the thin, many-jointed *kaatsin* and bent them around on either side of his head. Kyra still shuddered at the sight and immediately closed her eyes, tensing when she felt the hard tips move along her face and sucking in her breath as they pierced her skin.

After the moment of warm fuzziness that stopped the pain, Kyra called forth what she could remember of the day Antnee had taken the lock out of the door and attacked her and Marne. She felt more pieces come back to her, as well as the alien's confusion about the purpose of this exercise. It didn't matter; she knew what she wanted to remember. She requested that he give her some privacy with her memory. Kyra sensed his hurt feelings again, but felt him withdraw, leaving her to study the now-perfect mental reconstruction.

~Thank you,~ she told him, upon getting what she wanted from the memory. He carefully withdrew his *kaatsin*, healed the pinprick wounds, and folded the spindly limbs back into his neck. She half-watched in fascination at the insect-like movement of the appendages.

Marne said nothing; he didn't pry further, as she had requested. She settled back down, pulling the blankets over her shoulders. She sensed his curiosity and half-smiled.

~You can ask. I just wanted to remember alone without you telling me what I was remembering.~

Marne said nothing at first. She watched his face, unable to see his consternation but sensing it grind around like machine gears.

~Why that memory?~ he finally asked.

Kyra sat up a little, leaning on her elbow, ready to explain. ~After that first time you used your *kaatsin* on me, I felt more…things. More of what other people were thinking and what I was thinking, and it took me a while to be able to tell the difference.~

~I suppose… Humans aren't usually as empathic or telepathic as you are…even before I enhanced it.~

Kyra shook her head. ~No, that's not what I'm saying. That day, that day that Antnee was gonna hit me, you were trying to stop him even though it hurt you, and I knew it. And Lyza threatened to throw you in the ocean and drown you or sell you back… Alyce was crying and Antnee could have gone and hurt her and you weren't strong enough to help her, too. But I made up my mind. I knew that, if he did go after Alyce, I wasn't going to leave you so Lyza could take you. I wouldn't, no matter what, because I loved you.~

Marne's shock at her words silenced her for a moment. She tensed her lips, wounded that he didn't realize how much he meant to her.

~And then you collapsed. You couldn't hide your thoughts and you felt terrible, like you had failed. If he went for me again, you couldn't do anything. I felt bad, too, 'cuz I was thinking about not taking care of Alyce if you were gonna get hurt. I thought I was a horrible person.~

~Kyra! You're not—~ Marne began, but the girl shook her head once more.

She continued. ~And, when we were coming back from Caterbree, Mom was having leftover visions. She was seeing things…and I think she saw what was going to happen to

Dad. She was nicer to me then, nicer than she ever was. But...it was different...~ She took a ragged breath.

Marne tried to interrupt again. ~Kyra, no, no—~

The girl frowned, realizing she wasn't hiding any of her thoughts. ~It's not you or me that she's really mad at; it's her, Marne. She—she thinks she's a horrible person, like you did and like I did, and we hurt each other 'cuz of it. And we didn't mean to. Only, she hurts worse...because... because...~

~Kyra, you don't have to say it...~

~Not saying something doesn't make it go away or make it less true!~ she chided. ~When you talked like Daddy in her head, told her to take care of me and Alyce, I think—I think it made her think he'd hate her, and it made her afraid because she hated it, too. Hated what she felt, what she wished...~

~Kyra...~ Marne began, but his friend didn't even have to shake her head before he trailed off.

~She wished I hadn't come back...and that Daddy had. She just loved him more...~ Kyra bit her lip, then jumped when she felt Marne's two small hands wrap around her fingers. She looked down at him in surprise, and he stared up at her with his stone-black eyes. ~It's okay,~ she assured him. ~If I had to choose, I'd pick Daddy, too...but that's why she wants to send me away to school and sell you back to the market. We remind her that she loved Daddy more... and that we came back instead of him.~

Marne didn't sleep at all that night. As sunlight filtered through the room's curtains, unrest crept throughout his entire body. The whole plan was a foolish one, but he remembered Kyra's threat all too well.

~I'm going. Alone, if I have to.~

He would have taken it for an idle threat if he didn't know her, or, rather, himself, so well. She knew him well enough to know he wouldn't let her run away alone. And he knew she was stubborn enough to leave, knowing he'd follow. It wasn't a bluff, exactly, or maybe it was *her* calling *his* bluff. He didn't know, but he didn't like it either way.

He hadn't been on many planets, but he still felt certain that no planet was any place for a runaway eleven-year-old human, with or without a defective Naratsset.

He watched her silently through her morning routine: washing, dressing, going downstairs for breakfast, and returning angry at the small portion her family had allotted for him. Rather than chide her for likely getting herself into trouble for his sake, he turned his argument around. ~You do realize that, when we run away, we'll be missing more than a few meals. Portions will be the least of your worries.~

~You said you were going to do this with me.~

Marne sighed. ~I did, and I will. I'm just pointing out a problem.~

~We'll pack food, and when we find my granddad, he won't starve us.~

~Do you have a plan to find him?~

"Ah doo!" she replied proudly. The confidence worried Marne more than if she hadn't any plan. The girl grabbed her journal from its hiding place and opened it to a page where a leaf of paper fell out. Marne picked it up and read. It was a brochure for InterGalactic Travel Cruises, including a partial schedule and some notes in handwriting that wasn't Kyra's.

Marne looked up at her, not understanding this plan of hers.

She pointed to the writing and the ship circled. ~That's the ship we were taking when we met him. He was going to the next planet on that line for a while. It's only been a few months, so he's probably still there. We sneak onto an InterGalactic Travel Cruise and find him!~

Marne blinked twice. ~You want to sneak onto an InterGalactic Travel Cruise ship?~

"Yuh-es," she replied out loud.

~And how do you intend on doing that?~

~We'll figure it out when we get there. I remember Daddy saying how most of the security is just for show, anyway.~

Marne said nothing and returned to eating his small bowl of cereal.

"Whut do yoo think?" she asked.

His small mouth tensed. ~I said I'd go with you and stay with you, no matter what. It doesn't mean I think that this is, in any way, a good idea, Kyra.~

"Hmph!" the girl replied, standing up. He felt she wanted more support, but he couldn't honestly give any more. He watched in silence as she packed for their journey, carefully considering each item in her room.

Chapter 14
Boarding Call

MARNE'S STOMACH FELT as though a hundred razor-backed flies swarmed within as he watched Kyra tiptoe over to her sister's bed and kiss her goodbye. She whispered, "Ah love yoo. Ah'll come back. Ah promise, Aleece."

With that, she turned around and headed out her bedroom door. Marne followed closely behind, reaching up to hand her the money he'd "obtained" from Lyza's and Antnee's belongings. As far as he was concerned, it wasn't stealing—it was Kyra's rightful money they'd taken from her when they sold her books, her computers, and her future. She smiled at him, excited to embark upon their adventure.

For all his justified vengeance in getting Kyra's money, Marne did not share her enthusiasm as she unlocked her family's front door, walked through the stone gardens (their colors lost in the night's darkness), and onto their long, deserted road. Looking back at the house he'd begun to think of as home, he sighed. Then they headed into the Napoleon suburb toward the electrotram station.

Kyra's smile widened the closer they got to the e-tram station. It was nearly an hour's walk, and the night was clear. She looked hopefully up at the stars, wishing they would tell her that everything would be okay. But looking at them always made her happy, and she wasn't at all tired despite how late it was. An energy buzzed all the way from the top of her head and shoulders through her hands and into her whole body. She made herself hum noise through her mouth, like her grandfather had shown her. Marne looked at her oddly, and she stopped but smiled wider, wanting him not to worry so much. The thrill of leaving and being out late at night under the stars was what gave her so much energy, made her move her feet faster, she concluded. She didn't want to think about the thoughts Marne harbored of awful people waiting to hurt them...or the other e-tram ride—the one where the men had killed her father.

She refused to think of that now as she counted out the larger coins to purchase electrotram tickets from the automatic vendor. The sign next to the machine read that the IGT Cruise ships left from the stop listed as "Grand Port Board." Another sign talked about security checks and people having to turn their bags over if officers asked and how that was for everyone's own safety. Hoping they didn't run into any security officers, she bought one ticket for her and one for Marne, not remembering whether or not he needed his own ticket. She handed him the slip of plastic, and he regarded it curiously, even as he stayed on her heels all the way to the platform.

Because it was nighttime, the tram took longer to arrive. The ticket said that it could be a half-hour wait. Kyra stared out the several-story-high station windows, legs dangling from the bench. Marne sat beside her, his legs straight out, only the flat soles of his feet sticking over the edge. Now quiet and unmoving, Kyra got nervous. For his part, Marne didn't say anything, and she appreciated that. She was determined to see her plan through.

Feeling vibrations coming from the track, Kyra almost jumped from her seat. The alien looked at her worriedly, and she realized he didn't know what she was picking up. She motioned with her chin to the tracks and pressed her hand to the bench. Marne did the same but shook his head. Scrunching her lips, Kyra waited, feeling the tram coming closer and closer. It felt like it was going so slow. E-trams were fast, she knew, very fast. Shouldn't it be here by now?

Finally, Marne looked up, turning his antennae toward the left end of the tracks. Again, it seemed to take a long time, but it arrived, and it looked like it was slowing down from going very fast.

Sliding off her seat and clutching her ticket, Kyra made her way toward the doors. Only the front ones opened, so she headed there. The driver of the electrotram looked at her suspiciously. "Where's your parent?" he asked.

Kyra blinked, not thinking that this would be a problem.

"I'm calling security," he said. She gasped as the man reached for his radio; he was going to send her home!

In the same instant, Marne ducked his head forward and Kyra saw his *kaatsin* shoot up from his back—faster than she'd ever seen them move—and all point at the conductor. She felt him speak aloud even as he spoke in her head. "She's old enough that she doesn't need a parent. Let us on."

The conductor's eyes glazed over as though he were going to sleep, and he waved the two travelers aboard. Kyra stared in shock as Marne retracted his *kaatsin* as quickly as he'd extended them, before heading toward an empty corner of the e-tram.

~What did you *do* to him?~ she asked, and immediately wished she could take back the way she'd worded it.

He answered defensively, ~I didn't *do* anything *to* him. I just made him think you were old enough to travel alone.~

~You can *do* that?~

~Not often…and not well…and only if I use my *kaatsin*,~ he replied. ~And if anyone saw, they'd break them or kill me. As it is, we'll be lucky if no one stops us, because I don't have a repression collar.~

~What if someone did see you? What about the conductor? And what's a repression collar?~ Kyra glanced around in concern.

~There was no one else around,~ Marne assured her. ~And I made sure he didn't remember seeing me. And it's a collar we almost always have to wear so we can't use our powers on humans.~

Kyra considered that and nodded. ~I just don't want you to get hurt. And…~ She didn't know what to think or say about the collar.

He blew air out of his mouthslit, and she sensed he didn't want to talk about the collar. ~I told you, I've run away from places before. I know how to be careful.~

Kyra smiled at him and wanted to give him a hug, but saw him cringe when he picked up the thought, so she didn't touch him. She said, aloud, "Thank yoo, Marn-uh."

He looked at her for a long time and replied, ~Always.~

As they traveled, more and more people piled onto the tram-car. With each stop and each door opening, Marne held his breath until he scanned each entering person's surface thoughts. Kyra seemed far less nervous than he was, but Marne knew that she'd ridden on the e-tram a few times since she'd seen her father killed. The Naratsset had not.

Marne had had to climb into Kyra's lap two stops before "Grand Port Board," and was none too slow to hop off when the e-tram stopped—though he didn't stray far. He continued scanning as many surface thoughts as he could, though he felt the edges of fatigue creeping up on him from expending so much effort.

He sensed Kyra's hesitation as she balked at the doors, but people pushed from behind. The small human girl and his even smaller self found themselves thrown around like tiny boats in a sea of people. Marne fought to stay by Kyra's side, not quite ready to grab her hand to keep from separating, but considering it on more than one occasion.

They scanned the signs and drifted in the directions of arrows pointing toward interstellar travel. Marne felt his stomach clench at how many more signs warned about increased security and random checks. He looked for specific warnings about the UFC but found none. He hadn't seen any news since Nicolas had died; Lyza never put that on the wall-screen. What had happened after the attack?

As they left the platform and entered the station proper, the crush of people began to thin out, some going toward the merchant area, others to on-planet long-distance travel, and most toward Napoleon commuter trams. Kyra grabbed a pamphlet as they darted by a man sitting at an Information desk. Marne felt Kyra's heart fall, though, as she read the posted signs upon reaching the interstellar station.

She wasn't focusing on all the security signs that didn't say, specifically, who travelers needed to feel secure from. Instead, she was reading "No person under the age of 20 permitted without adult accompaniment" and "Pre-registration boarding pass required beyond this point," listed in all five of the major languages spoken on the planet

Cordelier, as well as another few that Marne recognized from high-commerce planets. Many of the signs, like the other security warnings, were shiny and new, and they all promised, "For your own safety." Marne understood almost all the written languages; Kyra understood three. Nevertheless, the message was the same.

Marne calculated out his age based on space travel and quickly came to the conclusion that the two of them, together, might exceed the age limit, but that didn't count. Besides, he wasn't considered a person, anyway. Regardless, they were also lacking a "pre-registration boarding pass."

~Now what do you want to do?~ he asked Kyra, who frowned as she looked around. She didn't answer directly, but he felt her desire to consider the situation. With a sigh, he also studied his surroundings.

"Hey, little girl. Little girl, are you lost?" came a voice from behind them. Marne turned around, seeing a middle-aged man with a suitcase come toward them. He sensed no ill thoughts from the person, but the event with the e-tram conductor was still fresh in his mind—and there were too many people here for him to use his *kaatsin*.

The Narratset alerted Kyra to the man's approach and communication. Kyra turned and smiled sweetly at the man. "Ah'm fine. Mah grandfather said tew waite heehr fohr heem. He'll be heehr shortlee."

The man considered her words and glanced between her and Marne in concern.

"Marnuh helps mee because Ai cayn't heehr," she explained, keeping her sweet smile turned on and pointing to her ears. "Ah'm okay, reelee. Thank yoo."

"Well, all right," he said, and headed toward the entrance. When his back turned, Kyra scrunched her lips and continued scanning the area with narrowed eyes, leaving

Marne to consider how frighteningly well his friend had lied to the stranger.

He sensed Kyra's mind upon the baggage area to their right, which stretched on both sides of the entrance booths. Not wanting to pry, he kept watch for any more well-intentioned persons who would present trouble. His black eyes glanced up at the large box of wall screens to their left.

"*Andakei!*" he cursed and thought sharply. Kyra turned around quickly; he pointed at the cube of wall-screens in the center of the port's foyer—all of which showed her face. On each side's bottom three screens scrolled her name, address, and contact information.

"Hey, that's the girl!" The well-meaning stranger turned back and pushed through people to get back to Kyra.

Kyra cursed as well, grabbed Marne's hand, and began to weave her own way around people and baggage. Marne protested at first, then realized he couldn't keep up with her at this speed—especially with her trying to get lost in the crowd. His small legs slowed her down, though, so he levitated, reducing the drag. She glanced behind her when she felt his lightness, and he winked at her. Smiling, she dragged the floating Naratsset back to the junction of the commuter trams and the merchant ones, where no wall-screens were immediately visible.

She slowed down, blending in with the people waiting for other trams. Leaning on one column, Kyra released Marne's hand and took a hooded shirt from her bag. It was a size too big, and the hood shadowed her face. It was the current trend, as well; Marne noticed a few people sporting similar styles. Some luck, he hoped.

Kyra took a few breaths and then reached for Marne's hand again. He balked, putting both hands behind his back.

~Sorry, Marne... Can you keep up?~ she asked him.

His mouthslit quivered as he considered. ~What, *exactly*, do you plan on doing?~

Crouching so she was almost eye-level with him, she relayed her plan. He tilted both his antennae inward, thinking; he had no better idea.

~I suppose.~

~Can you keep up with me, then, when we go back?~ she asked, her mental tone kinder.

Marne didn't answer right away. ~She's looking for you, obviously,~ he said finally. ~She wants you back, Kyra. She's probably worried about you.~

The girl frowned and shook her head. ~I'll let her know I'm okay when I get to Granddad.~

~Kyra——~

~Can you keep up?~ she asked, making it clear that returning home was not up for discussion.

Slowly, he reached out to her.

Kyra sent her appreciation for his trust as she gently took his hand.

They headed back toward the interstellar port. Kyra set a fast pace that matched most of the other people but took advantage of their smaller size to keep her weaving pattern until they reached the baggage carousel. A ship would be heading out within the hour, so the intercom system and lighted signs announced.

~What if it's going to the wrong planet?~ Marne asked quickly, as soon as she let go of his hand. Kyra shook her head, smiling almost smugly as she tapped a finger on a fresh paper pamphlet she'd grabbed at the interstellar port's entrance.

~It's leaving on the same schedule as the one we took before!~

~Okay,~ he replied as he turned his gaze to the baggage carousel and inspected the luggage and the people. One particularly crabby-looking woman placed a snap-suitcase on the loading belt, Marne noticed. Taking a deep breath, he concentrated upon it until it tipped and snapped open, spewing brightly colored clothes that quickly tangled and stopped the belt.

As Marne expected, the woman exploded in fury upon the staff, inciting several others to come to her aid. He glanced behind him and felt a moment of panic when his friend wasn't there. He looked at the access door that the guard had stepped away from. Kyra was already there, one hand on the knob, her other tracing the code buttons and card slider.

By the time he jogged over to her, she had managed to open the door much to Marne's surprise. How had she gotten the door open? He didn't see any key. Befoe he could ask, Kyra ducked in, holding the door open just long enough for Marne to slip behind her. No one was in the room, but someone could show up at any moment. Marne knew this and sensed her urgency.

Marne reached to open the next door with his mind. Kyra was already there; he felt her presence in the mechanics. Withdrawing his mind, he stared in further astonishment. She didn't seem to notice; her finger traced down the card slot and over the lock. He heard the *click* as it unlocked. She beckoned her confused friend to follow and led them down a long, narrow hallway. To their left, Marne could hear the whine-grind of the stuck carousel belt. They came to another door. Kyra opened it. The two stopped in their tracks.

"Look, there's nothing I can do on my end. I'm as stuck as you are!" A man with his back to the door spoke furiously into his communicator as he stared at the stopped baggage conveyor. Marne quickly led Kyra behind a pile of luggage, but the man didn't notice the door opening or their movement. The girl looked at Marne.

Marne sighed. He was exhausted. Nevertheless, she needed him. He found a wallet with a long, thin shoulder strap and grabbed it, then jerked his head to indicate she should follow him along the shadow's edge toward the ship.

~Breathe. But slowly,~ he told her, feeling pressure reflecting in his chest from her holding her breath.

Not far from where they had come in, several bags sat on the conveyor between a baggage opening in the ship's side and where the belt came through a large window. If they arched their necks out of the shadow, Kyra and Marne could see into the port they'd come from; Marne could still hear the woman yelling on the other side. Silently, he started twirling the wallet so he'd have enough momentum for the throw he needed to make.

The belt whined and shook rhythmically. Paying attention to the shakes, Marne focused on the farthest suitcase and twirled the wallet faster. With the next jolt of the belt, he let the wallet fly. It hit the suitcase, toppling it to the ground. It skidded to the far corner of the room.

The man cursed, talked into his radio again, and went over to grab the runaway suitcase. Marne grabbed Kyra's hand. The girl hadn't a moment to register surprise at his touch. Extending his *kaatsin* to help keep people from noticing him and Kyra—he'd never have enough energy to protect them if he didn't—he pulled her under the carousel belt and into the hole in the side of the ship. He tucked away his psychic appendages as quickly as he had taken them out.

Inside the luggage area was dark. Passengers claimed their belongings after the anti-grav takeoff, so now it was empty of persons and without light. Kyra took a few deep breaths and clutched Marne's hand.

~Not so tight!~ he scolded her.

~Sorry!~

He felt the panic in her psychic voice. She was already down one sense, and with the only light coming from the baggage hole—which they needed to avoid—the loss of sight filled her with terror.

~It'll be all right. You can...*hold*...my hand. I can see.~

~You can?~

~Yes. There's a door to the left.~

His assurance made a world of difference to her. She already trusted him to hear for her, Marne figured; seeing was only another step. Breathing easily, she kept her fingers just brushing his small palm as he led her to the door.

~No access to the keypad or card scan on this side... I can try...~

~I can do it,~ she told him. He sensed her pride and stepped away. She moved her hands, finding the edges of the door.

~Wait!~

Kyra pulled her hands back from the door with a start. ~What?~

~There's a person on the other side... They're walking by.~ Marne was silent for a few minutes. ~Now it's okay.~

Kyra took a deep breath. Marne sensed her trying to quiet her pounding heart. In a moment, the door opened. He heard her take another deep breath as they both scanned the hallway. ~Good,~ she thought to him. ~Now, if we can get to one of the *eqcannus* lounges, we'll be okay. We spent a bunch of time there when my family was on this before; they won't ask questions, and all that's on the wall-screens are the races and stuff about *eqcannuses*.~

~If you say so,~ Marne said. ~I really need to rest. I can't do much more if I don't.~

~We can rest there.~ She smiled and cautiously led the way.

Chapter 15
United Foundation Consortium

THE RACING AND gambling lounge had a few couches near the back. Kyra and Marne all but collapsed on one. The room was mostly empty, and other passengers had taken other couch seats and dozed, clutching bet sheets in their hands. Some kids sat with parents or napped, leaning on shoulders. Two or three very young children ran around in the other corner, which was decorated as a bright, padded castle. Marne had never seen a real castle, but Kyra had shown him pictures of the ones in the countryside of Angbritt, from when she was in New Cymru for her mother's starsinging.

Kyra used an armrest as a pillow and Marne curled up by her feet. He intended to only rest some, to keep watch while Kyra slept, but he was asleep before he even picked up her slumber.

He was awakened, too soon, by the near presence of another human. A woman, dressed in grey-and-white skirt and blouse with a silver name tag, was trying to wake Kyra.

"Excuse me, little girl, wake up... Aren't your parents worried about you?" she said softly, leaning just a little toward Kyra.

Kyra continued to sleep. The woman spoke louder and a few people on the other couches began to take notice.

"She's deaf," Marne explained, forcing himself awake and somewhat alert while poking Kyra with his toes to wake her. "Her parents were going to grab luggage...and meet her here... I think—she loves watching the *eqcannus*—so they sent me with her... We must have dozed."

"You've been here for three hours," the woman replied, eyes narrowing suspiciously. Marne knew she was looking for his repression collar or some sort of a lead.

"Yoo're s'pohsed t'wayke me up sooner!" Kyra chastised her friend as she sat up. Her tone and words shocked him to silence. He didn't have time to read her mind before she continued, "Wee're s'pohsed t'meet mum aynd dad at the upper breakfust fayve minnets ago!" She looked up at the woman. "Sohry... Please 'scuse us!"

The woman frowned, unsure. "Well, you better hurry," she said, speaking slowly and uncomfortably.

Kyra nodded. "Thank yoo for wayking us." She turned back to Marne with a sharp eye. "Come ohn! Wee have to huhrry!"

Marne felt her pour a stream of mental apologies toward him, even as he sensed the woman's acceptance of Kyra's chastisement. Just to make the situation more credible, he asked Kyra to take his hand. While he felt her surprise, she didn't show it, taking his small fingers sharply, as though she were furious and worried he'd run away.

As she "dragged" him out, Marne turned one antenna on the woman. She had pulled out her communicator and was banging it on her hand. The Naratsset could hear only static from it. Finally, she cursed and returned the comm to her belt and started gathering glasses from a nearby table.

When they finally left the lounge entirely, he interrupted the stream of "I'm sorry" that Kyra continued to think at him and said, ~No. You did good. That's what the woman needed to see.~

~But you're upset!~

Marne paused, realizing that she had read him truly. ~I'm upset…that you…lie so well. I wish you didn't have to. You always say you don't lie…and the thing…what your dad said…and what you said?~

Kyra pursed her lips and didn't reply right away. ~I know. But what else could I do? We would get sent back home and worse things would happen.~ After a moment, she added, ~Besides, they're not friends or family. They're not people I love.~

Marne hadn't any words to send her, but he opened himself so she could feel his returned emotions.

After she seemed to lead him down a number of hallways, he finally asked, ~Where are we going?~

~Lower food deck. It's open all day and you just pick up the food you want.~

~Oh.~ He'd never been on one of these ships before, at least not outside of the live cargo area. He trusted she knew where she was going. Something else played on his still-sleepy mind, though. ~The thing you do to the doors… I didn't know you could do that!~

She smiled widely and lifted her chin proudly. He picked up her memory of their conversation on the e-tram, her surprise at his abilities.

Marne sighed. ~Okay, so there was no earlier reason for you to show me, I get it. How do you do it, though? It's not like my powers.~

Kyra hesitated, then shrugged honestly. ~I just do. I'm good at fixing things so they work for me, stuff with wires. I think 'cuz my hands are sensitive, I feel wires, and I can make the wires work for me.~

~Wires?~ Marne asked.

Kyra shrugged again and nodded toward a sliding door that opened as they approached.

The alien's antennae twitched and wriggled at the tantalizing smells of food that reached through his tired brain. He smelled something else, too, something he knew was familiar but didn't recognize right away. Dulling his awareness of their surroundings a little, he continued to wrap his mind around his friend's abilities. ~Are you sure it's the wires? Maybe it's the currents, or waves—that's got to be it. All electrical devices emit waves, like sound. You feel it when people talk or yell—maybe you can feel the electricity or the magnetic pulse—all types of waves, even! And you can manipulate them!~

~I guess,~ came her reply, not holding the same excitement as Marne. She reached to take two plates from a station as they entered.

~Don't you see how—~ Marne stopped mid-thought. He recognized the scent now. It was stronger in here. He looked around anxiously, ignoring her mind in his for a moment.

"How whut?" Kyra muttered when Marne didn't finish his question. "Marn-uh?"

He sent her a wordless warning. She immediately glanced around and noticed what he did, that everyone was looking at them!

~Marne!!~ she mentally shouted.

Two guards stood at the door, holding what Marne recognized as dual discharge guns. The weapons allowed the shooter to use either energy blasts or physical bullets.

However, it was not the guns that filled both of them with terror, but the insignia upon the sides of the guns.

A three-pointed blue star in an orange-and-gold circle was burned in Marne's mind from that day on the tram. The same insignia worn by the people who'd killed Kyra's father. The terrorists.

The United Foundation Consortium.

Chapter 16
The Star's Lessons

"WHOSE LITTLE GIRL are you?" asked a gunman in Common Cordelieran.

Kyra's mouth moved but no sound came out. For the better, Marne thought, as he piped in. "Seinnat," he said, picking a name he knew to be pretty common in Napoleon. "She's deaf…and mute." *And numb*, he acknowledged fearfully.

The soldier spoke into a radio in a language Marne didn't know well, and he couldn't concentrate enough to decipher it. He just picked up the name Seinnat. They must be checking the registry. What was going on?

With the end of his gun, the talking soldier gestured for them to sit at a nearby table. Kyra didn't respond; Marne could feel her shutting down, freezing. He took her hand and led her there. Once she was seated, albeit on the edge of a chair, the Naratsset looked around to digest the situation.

Small food-bearing robots stood still. No one was eating. In the far corner behind where he and Kyra sat, Marne saw about ten dead bodies piled. That smell, the smell of human blood, was what had caught his attention. He kept the sickening realization closed in his mind; he didn't want Kyra to have to experience it.

Most of the hostages' eyes now returned to the two soldiers at the doors. They seemed to be calling the shots. Other UFC gunmen and women stood around a group of people in the center, keeping them, specifically, at gunpoint. Marne recognized the faces of high-level politicians from Cordelier; he'd seen them at Nicolas's funeral as well as on many of Napoleon's newscasts. Some uniformed medics cared for one of them. The ones in the corner had probably been their guards.

He looked back at Kyra. Her green eyes were almost covered with panic-widened pupils, black as his eyes. This wouldn't do; the storm of her mind felt too similar to Zalana's.

~Kyra! Kyra! Kyra!~ he shouted into her mind, but it felt like throwing rocks into a wall. She hurt too much; her memories had flooded back to her consciousness. He didn't know what to do.

They sat for several minutes. The leftmost door guard continued to speak into his radio. Marne focused enough to decipher that they were affirmatively listing checkpoints secured around the vessel. Finally, he recognized the name Seinnat, and the soldier began to shake his head.

~Kyra! Wake up!~

No reply, no register, nothing.

The guard walked over.

"There are no families named Seinnat missing children." He shouldered the rifle and pulled his sidearm, another type of blaster with the same insignia. Marne didn't have to read his mind to know he'd kill either of them with hardly a thought. "Who is the little girl, Ratsi? Who are you protecting?"

"Maybe…maybe it's under her mother's name…or a mix-up in registration?" he suggested, psychically shouting at Kyra, trying to wake her from her mental stupor.

The soldier shook his head and shoved the smaller blaster in his face. Kyra gasped. Marne took some small comfort in that his impending death had pulled Kyra into alertness, but he doubted it would do any good at this point.

The radio crackled again. The man spoke in his foreign tongue. Both Kyra and Marne understood one key word in the conversation.

Starbard.

The soldier turned his gun toward Kyra.

The girl grabbed the barrel of the soldier's gun with both hands. Neither he nor Marne had expected such a bold move. There was an explosion of light, and the gun shattered back into the guard's chest. Kyra shrieked as the energy coursing through the remnants of the gun barrel burned her hands and threw her backward.

Immediate chaos followed. Believing the soldiers had fired upon the child, the crowd mobbed the attackers.

~Now's our chance,~ Marne mentally yelled at her. He scanned the area. ~The robot door!~ He pointed.

Ray blasts streaked around them.

Kyra crawled on wrists and knees toward the food-service robot door, then stopped halfway there. With a pained grimace, she placed her hand on the metal runners the robots followed.

~What are you doing?~ Marne demanded.

~Watch,~ she said. The robots jumped to life. Zipping around, throwing the food they carried, they added to the confusion. Tables fell over, giving Kyra and Marne cover.

Unfortunately, one soldier spotted their escape route and met them at the robot door, pistol-blaster ready.

~Just go!~ Marne yelled at Kyra, throwing up the same type of energy shield he'd used against Antnee.

The soldier fired. Marne's barrier held, but he was knocked into Kyra. They slipped into the kitchen just in front of a robot.

Kyra's reddened hand was on the robot rail once more. The machine, slightly taller than Marne, stopped, keeping soldiers from following them through.

~Hold on,~ Marne said as she got to her knees. He crawled up her back and clutched her pack. ~I can't keep up if you run...and you might need both hands for stuff.~

Stray blasts flew through the robot entry. Kyra backed away. There were three doors in the kitchen.

Marne pointed to the one directly in front of them. ~People coming that way.~

She ran to the closest door on her right. As she touched it, she shivered. ~Freezer,~ she declared.

Swallowing hard, she placed her hands on the other door. Marne clung to her backpack, eyes on the third door. He could now hear the sounds of approach. A whir and a breeze told him Kyra had gotten the desired door open. Behind was a locker-and-dressing area. No one was inside. Some of the lockers were still open, clothing spilling onto the floor.

~Can you fix the door so they can't open it right away?~ Marne suggested.

She bit her lip and pressed her shaking and swollen fingers to the keypad as the door closed. ~Maybe. Don't know if it'll work.~

~Worth a try,~ Marne said, looking over her head.

Kyra dashed around the locker room, and Marne struggled to find his bearings as he rode her backpack. After a few turns, they located the emergency exit.

~They'll expect an alarm,~ she explained. Marne could feel perspiration rise from her head as she disarmed their escape door. She paused once to wipe sweat from her face with her sleeve.

The door silently opened outward. Kyra went through and dealt with that side's alarm lock. The door closed, and the red light above it re-lit. She sighed, wiped her face again, gingerly flexed her hands, and continued down the hallway.

Then Marne heard the intercom and froze, tugging on Kyra's pigtails for her attention.

"This ship is now under the control of the United Foundation Consortium," came a male voice over the ship's intercom. "Please remain calm and stay where you are, and no one else will get hurt. We will be detouring the *Treasure Ark* to Omnus, our station in the Alicorn Belt, to begin negotiations with Napoleon Cordelier United. Once again, this ship is now under the control of the United Foundation Consortium. Please remain calm…"

Marne transmitted what he heard to Kyra. He felt the bitterness as she thought the name of their enemies, the ones who had killed her father: ~United Foundation Consortium.~

Marne had no response. He stroked her hair gently, hoping she understood how he felt.

Kyra trembled and nodded, then continued to creep down the hall. "Mmn," the girl murmured softly, spotting a map on the left wall. She pointed to the closest set of escape pods.

~They probably already closed that off,~ Marne said. ~Or at least have it guarded.~

~They're going to kill us anyway,~ Kyra replied, ~and they don't know I disarmed the alarm, so they wouldn't have the most people looking in that section. Could you make another shield like you did in the cafeteria?~

Marne blew air through his mouthslit. He hoped so. ~Not for long and not very strong.~

~Just enough for cover while I get to a pod? Pods are just for one or two people, so taking one shouldn't be too hard. We don't need an escape ship.~

Marne gave no answer except for sentiments of disagreement, which Kyra ignored.

Kyra moved quickly but carefully, though neither she nor Marne sensed anyone nearby. The Naratsset could still hear the announcement over the intercom. It had gotten longer, explaining how hostages would be returned to their rooms and how the UFC would be overriding the locking systems, entrapping them until they reached Omnus. The message further explained that the hostages would be well taken care of during the negotiations with the planet Cordelier. It did not say, Marne noted, what would happen to the hostages if Cordelier did not cooperate.

Staying close to the wall, Kyra slowed as they approached the hall of escape ships and pods.

~Four. There's four guards. Two close. Right around the corner there,~ Marne informed her.

Kyra paused at the corner, thinking, then took several steps back. Before he could ask her what she was doing, she asked Marne, ~You can see in the dark, right?~

~Low light, not complete darkness.~

~Good enough. I think there's emergency lighting.~ Her fingers moved around a panel in the wall. She pried it open. The Naratsset winced at the pop.

Kyra flicked all of the switches behind the panel. The section's lights went out just as the nearest guards turned the corner. Kyra stooped low and rushed the closest one. The impact nearly threw Marne off her back, but it surprised the guard enough that she staggered a step back, buying the two runaways hardly a moment. Kyra traced the wall to keep course as she ran to the closest pod.

Marne threw up his shield immediately after the collision with the guard. Blue light dimly glowed from the edges of the floor and ceiling. Two energy blasts slammed into the shield. Kyra stumbled but kept going. The guards shouted to each other as they entered the hall with the escape pods.

One soldier was close enough to fire a few more rounds with a sidearm. Kyra moved fast, though. As she skidded to a stop at the closest pod, Marne heard the guards' running footfalls.

~Hurry!~ he warned. Maintaining a full energy shield for even those few seconds made his head throb, dulling his vision and hearing.

Kyra didn't reply.

The memory of Nicolas's dying face frightened the Naratsset and hurt enough to lend him strength. He hadn't reacted fast enough then. He hadn't been strong enough; he couldn't protect both of them then. As his pain and fatigue increased, he worried for Kyra.

The two closest guards were upon them and grabbed for the pair. Marne's shield zapped them with a psychic pulse, and they flew back several feet, hitting the floor.

More shouts echoed; Marne couldn't make them out. From the corner of his blurred vision, he saw the two he had zapped begin to retreat, yelling into their comms. Once they were around the corner, the other two guards fired. The impact on his shield told him the settings were lethal.

Marne could barely form Kyra's name when he felt his shield give.

Two sets of doors opened to the pod.

Escape from Unified
Foundation Consortium

Kyra jumped inside. She tossed Marne and her backpack to the closest chair.

~CLOSE THE DOORS!~ Marne psychically shouted, dizzy and nauseous from exertion. A blast came in through the doors, just missing Kyra and striking the back of the pod. Another quickly followed, grazing the console and setting off a shower of sparks. Still gripping the backpack, Marne ducked for cover under the seat.

~I AM!~ Kyra punched buttons on the control pad, punctuating each touch with a verbal "ow!"

The inner doors slid shut with a *hiss.*

An emotionless computer voice informed them that life support was engaged and they needed to begin the repulsion sequence. Marne transmitted this to Kyra. She nodded, sitting in the upright control chair.

Tears filled her eyes as she shook her head at the sparking console. More blasts shook the sealed doors and began to make dents. Marne choked on his breath, realizing the doors to the hallway must still be open.

"Please begin repulsion sequence. Pod sustaining damage to atmospheric seals," said the disembodied pod voice.

Kyra stared at Marne, agape, when he transmitted that. He knew that her father had taught her enough about space travel for her to understand the consequences to the *Treasure Ark* if they took off and left the ship's atmospheric doors open…and she definitely realized consequences to the two of them if they didn't take off soon.

Another blast carved a deep dent right beside the atmospheric seal to the door.

~Just make it go! Release the pod and go!~ Marne ordered.

~They'll all get sucked into space and die!~

~They want to kill you and me... They killed your father——~ He stopped. True as all that was, it hurt to say, to think, to realize what he was saying.

Kyra frowned. ~That doesn't make it right.~

She balanced on the chair's edge and slowly passed her hands over the console and the buttons. The sparks calmed and stopped.

The bangs and dents did not. The guards now aimed for the atmospheric seals.

~Kyra, just one hole——~

~I know.~ Tears streamed down her face. She adjusted the controls and a text scroll started on one of the screens the blasters hadn't cracked. She sat silently for a half second's eternity. Marne watched.

He couldn't do anything else.

She punched more buttons and read the screen. The computer vocalized the tiny print he could see her scanning. It must have sounded outside, as well; the banging paused. "Pod hall III containment commencing. Atmospheric doors descending."

A few more frenzied bangs hit the pod, but not as hard. Apparently the guards weren't suicidal, Marne thought. Kyra hardly seemed to notice; she hit a few more buttons, still flinching with each jab.

"Repulsion sequence commencing. Please, for your safety, fasten security harnesses for EM repulsion."

Kyra grabbed Marne before he could react. As she buckled him to her chest, he realized he hadn't the energy to react, anyway. The pod pushed away from the *Treasure Ark*.

The computer voice and a violent hissing told Marne he had more to worry about than being squashed against a human in a security harness.

"Atmospheric seals compromised. Life support compromised. Oxygen levels dropping."

Kyra must have read the same thing, because she audibly mimicked one of the curse words he used. She unbuckled so she could lean directly over the console. Marne slid from her lap. She moved her hand over every button and switch, trying to find something, anything that would help. Marne shakily crawled around the floor. He'd been on short-jumpers before, small crafts. There was always a seal kit; there had to be one here.

~Kyra!~ he sent, using all of his weight to barely budge a small box from under the rear chair. She scrambled over and helped pull out the kit: a palm-sized magnetic generator that created an airtight force-shield that Marne knew put his to shame on his best day.

Since it was electronic, it took Kyra little effort to employ it. Marne collapsed onto the box, losing the battle against fatigue. In a few moments, she scooped him back up and re-harnessed them. With half-open eyes, he watched as she activated a view; the appearance of metal gave way to stars.

"Mmnnhmmm," Kyra murmured aloud.

Marne twisted in the belts to look up at her. ~Kyra?~ He stopped short of asking if she could hear them. But he felt something in her mind. Like the static drums he'd felt when she was a planet away, only clearer. She looked utterly entranced as she stared into the space surrounding them.

~They really are talking to me,~ she said. ~I—I saw this. After Mom starsang and I couldn't get to sleep. I wrote it in my journal, but every time I read it, I felt sick. Or something. But I dreamed of exactly this! You. And me. Like this… The stars all around us. And I can feel the song, like when Mom sings, but it's just you and me here. Daddy and Granddad were right… They said I'd starsing in my own way. Maybe I will!~

~Do you know what they're saying now?~ he asked, letting alone the fact he'd told her the very same thing.

She paused. ~No... I don't know how I did it before. It might have been because Mom did the starsinging. But... but I will someday. I can...*feel* them saying so.~

After a moment's pause, she inspected the life support and oxygen levels. With a dejected sigh, she set their course back to Cordelier. With their remaining oxygen level, they would never make it to Caterbree, much less any other life-supporting planet. But they were safe for now. Marne had kept her safe.

~Are you going home, then?~ Marne asked.

~We're going back to Cordelier, but we aren't going home. We can't make it safely anywhere else with our life support levels.~

Marne sensed her putting together another plan, but he was too weak to focus on her thoughts. Except for one. "Home" was where they would end up, but home wasn't on Cordelier. Not for Kyra anymore.

~Home is safe. With you. My best friend.~

Marne swallowed, overcome with emotion.

Kyra, his best friend, looked back up to the stars. Marne remembered her relaying how her mother described the sound of the stars: the life-beat of everything or something like that. He could feel Kyra's heartbeat through her clothing. More than the drumming static he sensed in her head. Did she sense the stars like the beats of a heart? Her sharp mind picked up his unspoken question.

~Yes... It's kind of like that. Heartbeats. But millions... or more...zillions...~

Surrounded by zillions of sparkling heartbeats singing a questionable future neither of them could yet decipher, Marne let himself fall asleep to the sound of the only heartbeat he really cared about.

The only one he'd follow across the stars or back to an unwelcoming planet, on the most foolish plan imaginable, because he would do anything to keep it beating.

The only heartbeat...

Acknowledgements

While Kyra may be all but an orphan by the end of *Silent Starsong*, she has a huge family in my world.

First and foremost, thank you to my amazing husband and soul mate, Scott, who still loves Kyra and Marne above all my other characters. Besides always being there to support me in my crazy writing adventures, he's especially been there for Kyra's adventures. Thank you, my dearest!

Also—many, many thanks to my wonderful family who has always been supportive and loving, no matter what. I really have been blessed when it comes to all of you.

Very special thanks to my Spencer Hill Press family who helped me bring Kyra to publication. Jenn Carson, you have super-magical abilities when it comes to the merciless slaying of excess verbiage—while still keeping my meaning. You also challenged me to share even more of Kyra's and Marne's worlds and all the people and cultures who live there… which made me so happy that Scott was sick of hearing me say, "She said I could write MORE!" Sunder Addams, you were a great first copyeditor who continued to challenge me to write better, stronger, more concisely, and more accurately. Shecky, your grammar details and nit-picking of small-yet-still-very-important things gave *Starsong* the shine and glimmer it needed. Rich "Platinum" Storrs, you've been a dear friend to me through many SHP adventures; your tough comments, as always, make a stronger book— and that made earning your praise comments even more inspirational. Jenn AP, there are more thanks than can be said here, but thank you for letting me count on you for so much beyond just the publicity of my book. Veronica Jones, YOU PULLED THE CHARACTERS RIGHT OUT OF MY HEAD AND PUT THEM ON MY COVER! I did, literally, cry. Especially when I saw my Marne *real!* And Slake Saunders, OMG—your internal art is so, so perfect! I cried some more! Last, but far from least, Kate Kaynak, none of our dreams would be hung among the stars were it not for your support, love, and trust. Thank you!

Even before Kyra and Marne arrived at Spencer Hill Press, they received a lot of love and feedback from many people. Del, thank you for the massive amounts of love and support...even to the extent of my own husband. Hearing your cheers at every step of my career have kept me moving closer and closer to the stars. Thank you to my DragonWriter colleagues, Sunder among you; when my idea for Kyra and Marne arrived and I didn't have time to write them, you refused to let me give them up...and you critiqued and strengthened my very earliest drafts with the impossible space physics and contradictory culture-building. Ann Crispin, wherever you are among the heavens, I hope you can see how much both your critique and your support of my workshop submissions made this a better story and gave me the confidence I needed. Thank you. Renée and Sean, I lost count of how many times you offered your dining-room table or studio for me to escape and get edits done, but those visits helped more ways than I can tell. Aimee Weinstein, you are always an excellent beta reader and supporter. Ellen Shetler, thank you for the information on music and the deaf. To my Southbridge writers group, who have also been seeing pieces of Kyra's world for many, many years, your continual feedback over many so many drafts is so much appreciated!

I know there are more of you, so please forgive me. I've sung your praises to the stars and will continue to do so.

Thank you again.

And again.

Also by T.J. Wooldridge

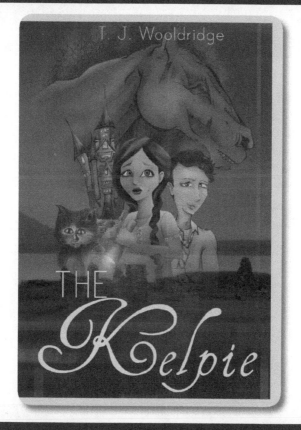

When Heather and Joe decide to be Sleuthy MacSleuths on the property abutting the castle Heather's family lives in, neither expected to discover the real reason children were going missing:

A Kelpie. A child-eating faerie horse had moved into the loch "next door."

SPENCER HILL MIDDLE GRADE

Real Girls Don't Rust † Real Girls Don't Rust † Real Girls Don't Rust † Re
n't Rust † Real Girls Don't Rust † Real Girls Don't Rust † Real Girls Don't
s Don't Rust † Real Girls Don't Rust † Real Girls Don't Rust † Real Girls Do

Steampunk anthology of seven short
stories ranging from reimagined folk
tales to unique alternate histories.

st † Real Girls Don't Rust † Real Girls Don't Rust † Real Girls Don't Rust † Re
on't Rust † Real Girls Don't Rust † Real Girls Don't Rust † Real Girls Don't
eal Girls Don
ust † Real G   Real Gir
on't Rust †   st † Re
irls Don't Rus   on't Rust
Real Girls Do   Girls Do
ust † Real G   Real Gir
on't Rust †   st † Re
irls Don't Rus   on't Rust
Real Girls Do   Girls Do
ust † Real G   Real Gir
on't Rust †   st † Re
irls Don't Rus   s Don't
eal Girls Don   Real Gir
ust † Real G   st † Re
on't Rust †   on't Rust
irls Don't Rus   Girls Do
Real Girls Do   Real Gir
ust † Real G   st † Re
on't Rust †   on't Rust
irls Don't Rus   Girls Do
Real Girls Do   Real Gir

Real Girls Don't Rust

Edited by Jennifer Carson

Real Girls Do   Real Gir
ust † Real Girls Don't Rust † Real Girls Don't Rust † Real Girls Don't Rust † Re
on't Rust † Real Girls Don't Rust † Real Girls Don't Rust † Real Girls Don't Rust
irls Don't Rust † Real Girls Don't Rust † Real Girls Don't Rust † Real Girls Do

SPENCER HILL MIDDLE GRADE

Real Girls Do   Real Gir
ust † Real Girls Don't Rust † Real Girls Don't Rust † Real Girls Don't Rust † Re
on't Rust † Real Girls Don't Rust † Real Girls Don't Rust † Real Girls Don't Rust
irls Don't Rust † Real Girls Don't Rust † Real Girls Don't Rust † Real Girls Do
Real Girls Don't Rust † Real Girls Don't Rust † Real Girls Don't Rust † Real Gir
ust † Real Girls † Real Girls Don't Rust † Real Girls Don't Rust † Real Gir
Real Girls † Real Girls Don't Rust † Real Girls Don't Rust † Real Girls Don't

AUGUST 2013

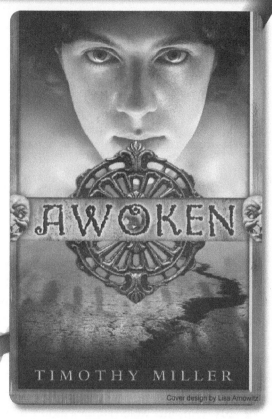

AWOKEN

TIMOTHY MILLER

Cover design by Lisa Amowitz

Fourteen-year-old boy discovers elemental powers
and is caught in a war between frightening dollmen
and a more frightening corporation that would use
his powers to redefine "human."

SPENCER HILL MIDDLE GRADE

About the Author

T.J. Wooldridge is the child-friendly persona of Trisha J. Wooldridge, who reviews dining establishments in Faerie for her local Worcester-area paper (much to all the natives' confusion) and writes grown-up horror short stories that occasionally win awards (EPIC 2008, 2009 for anthologies Bad-Ass Faeries 2 and Bad-Ass Faeries 3). Her novels include *The Kelpie* (December 2013) and *The Earl's Childe* (December 2014) in the MacArthur Family Chronicles, and *Silent Starsong* (July 2014) in the Adventures of Kyra Starbard series. During not-writing moments, she enjoys the following activities: spending time with her Husband-of-Awesome, a silly tabby cat, and two Giant Baby Bunnies in their Massachusetts home; reading; riding her horse in the nearby country stables and trails (not very well); reading Tarot (very well); drawing (also not very well); making jewelry (pretty well); making lists; and adding parenthetical commentary during random conversations.